LAST CALL

Serg Koren

Cover image by Gorbash Varvara/Shutterstock.com

Last Call

ISBN: 978-1-09839-288-8

Other books by Serg Koren:

- Puffin and Griswold In The Tunnel Of Darkness
- The Roland Targus Series
  - The Treasure
  - The Curse
  - The Kingdom
  - The Couple

For everyone.

1

Water rushes out of my nose and lungs as I gag and cough on the banks of the Anacostia just outside of D.C. The raindrops make plunking noises as they hit the river's surface. I groan and roll over onto my back. That's a mistake. The throbbing in my head is out of rhythm with the rain that hits me as I stare into the black night sky. It's cloudy, just like my mind. I sit up feeling drunk but don't remember drinking. Staggering upright, I walk up the muddy bank and scan the area. I head for the distant glow of D.C. The path I follow is unpaved and deserted. A half hour later I find a road and start thumbing a ride. There aren't many cars and those that pass don't stop. I walk a couple of miles outside of town and luck out when a yellow pulls up.

"Where to?" The cabbie throws me a glance as I climb into the back. The toothpick in his mouth springs to attention when the burly man catches sight of me."You look like you've been dragged through the mud."

"Close enough." I grumble then give him the address to the room I'm renting.

"Sure you don't want a hospital, bud?"

"I'm fine. I just need a shower."

"Suit yourself, but I bet you feel worse than you look. I was just on my way home. Lucky I spotted you. Not much call for a cab this time of night."

"What time is it?"

"Just past one in the morning. So what happened, if you don't mind me askin'."

"Someone didn't like me asking questions. They didn't like me or the questions and dumped me in the river."

"Oh? You a cop? Or a private dick?"

"No, just a reporter."

"So who did it? You know?"

"I have a pretty good idea."

"I always wanted to be a reporter."

"Really?" I'm not that interested, but I am fighting to stay conscious and think conversation will help.

"Nah, not really." The cabbie guffaws. The toothpick in his mouth bobs up and down. "People open up if I tell them I want to be whatever they are. What I really wanted to be was a cowboy. But there's no call for those nowadays," he explains with a sigh. The car hits a hole in the road and the cabbie curses as he tries to keep the cab straight. "You'd think they'd fix roads in this day and age. Name's Cam by the way. So how many were there?"

"I'm Randy—Randy Cook. Not sure. More than one I think, if you don't count the dame."

Cam glances up at me through the rear-view mirror. "There's always a dame. Looker?"

"Yeah. She was in on it. I'm certain. But she couldn't have dragged me into the river without help." I pause. I hadn't thought it through. Why would anyone want to kill me? I was just doing a fluff story on the new art scene in D.C. Oncoming headlights approach and pass us on the left. Cam raises a hand to wave at the driver and his ring grabs my attention. An image flashes across my mind of a signet ring, but flat-faced.

"The ring," I blurt.

"Oh, this? What about it?" He holds the hand up. "It's my wedding ring. I still wear it even though we broke up. You know how that goes." The hand drops and Cam shrugs. "We didn't get along. Irreconcilable differences is what the lawyer said. Me? I just think we argued too much."

"Sorry to hear," I say, but my thoughts are on the strange ring. Just before I passed out, I glimpsed it. Whoever wore it had thrown me over their shoulder and into the river. I am sure of that.

"Glad we didn't have kids." I realize Cam is still talking. "It makes the breakup easier, you know?"

"Uh, huh."

"It's not like I had a lot invested in the relationship." He pauses. "It still hurts sometimes." The toothpick flinches. "I've been looking for a side-gig. What with the economy the way it is money is tight. Good thing we broke up on good terms."

I focus back on the conversation. "It's a rough world. You're lucky, you have a steady job. A lot of people are still out of work and most are struggling."

"I know. I guess you're safe. There's always news to report, right?"

"I think so. I get a lot of fluff; pet shows, art shows, and comings out."

"Hey that's what sells. Right?"

"I guess. I want to do some hard-hitting reporting."

"So why don't you?"

I shrug in the back seat. A bolt of lighting lights up the cab a moment too late to illuminate my gesture. The cab swerves. I grab the edge of the seat.

"Damn! I don't like lighting. It always makes me jump." I see Cam shake his head. His image in the review-view mirror is focused on the road. The toothpick is halfway into his mouth.

"Maybe you shouldn't drive in a storm."

"I don't mind rain. It's the lighting and thunder. They give me the creeps." He drives in silence. We've run out of small-talk. Or so I think. "So who do you work for?", he asks.

"The Herald—Washington Court House Herald."

The cabbie grunts in acknowledgment. "Here you go. Randy, you said your name was, right?" I glance at the meter. "If you need a cab, just ask for me, Cam. There's only one of me." He laughs as he pulls the cab alongside the curb of the cobblestone building where I live. I hand over the fare and throw in a fiver. At least they didn't take my wallet.

"Thanks!" Cam exclaims."It's a little soggy, but the banks will take it."

2

The next evening I feel clean and rested, at least physically. Someone had dumped me into the Anacostia. I had the when and where. I wanted to know who and why. A good journalist would find the answers. There was a story there, and I was the victim.

It's dark and pours sheets of rain. I trudge the couple of miles to Number 3 Green Court. Last night I had been drunk. I don't get drunk. I fight the rain that flails me from the sky as I enter the alley. The summers in D.C. are hot and humid. Now, the rains had come and mirror my dark mood. The nondescript entrance in front of me has a small sign and a large man. The sign reads "Abandon soap all ye who enter here." It's an attempt at humor I don't get. The man stands under an overhang shielded from the rain. He's dressed in an immaculate suit one size smaller than what he should have been wearing. His eyebrows shoot up then fall.

"Welcome back. I forget, you a cop or a Fed?"

"Neither. I'm just here to have some fun."

The large man looks at me. "Didn't you say you was a reporter."

"It must have been someone else. I'm not wearing my reporter hat tonight."

The giant grunts."You know the drill. No cops. No Feds. No guns." He pats me down. I flinch as he searches my nether regions. "You're clean. Stay that way and you won't get hassled. And don't ask questions." He tilts his head and I take that as a sign I can go in. He eyes me as I nod and enter the unassuming door.

The sound of a three-piece band trying to do a good version of Bessie Smith's "Sweet Georgia Brown" assails me. The smoke obscures

4

the gaudy art that hangs on the walls. Most of it is what passes for modern: shapes and paintings of naked women adorn the walls. I don't get it but it is au courant. I pass through the haze and din to the tall cedar of a man that stands behind a dark ornately carved desk that acts as the bar. But bars are illegal. This is an art gallery that serves if you know how to ask. The lanky tree nods. "What can I get you? I have soda, coffee, and tea."

"I want the good stuff." My voice is easy.

"We don't sell that. It's illegal, you know." The tree's eyes dart from side to side.

"Come on. Be a pal. I need something uh more interesting." I drop a fiver on the bar. "I had a rough day."

The man grabs the bill and pours a glass of clear liquid. "Here's your water, sir." Then he whispers. "It's water here. Got it?"

I nod. "What do you call water, then?"

He looks stumped, then responds. "No one orders water—unless it's water." He hisses, "Got it."

"Sure thing."

"You a cop?"

"No."

"You a dick?"

"No."

"No Feds allowed here."

"I'm not a Fed. I'm just a guy."

"What do you want?"

"Can't a guy just come here to relax?" I pause, then add, "And to enjoy the art? What do I call you?"

The man blinks hard. "Moe Reynolds"

"So you own the joint?"

"Nah. I just serve drinks."

I nod. "I was here last night. There was a number…"

He eyes me with suspicion. "Yeah. Tayla. What about her?"

"Yeah, her. I was just wondering where she is tonight?"

"Around. Why?"

"Oh, we just hit it off." That was half a lie. I wasn't sure I'd have to bring it up during my next confession. She and the ring are the only leads I have.

"Well Mac, I would stay away from her if I were you."

"Is that a threat?"

Moe takes a step back with his hands raised. "No. No. Of course not.

I'm just sayin' she has a boyfriend."

"You?"

His laugh is uneasy. "Me? Nah. I wish. Tayla's Goodwin Dolby's."

"The Congressman?"

Moe nods. "The one and only."

"When's Tayla here? Usually?"

Moe shrugs. "It's up to her. I don't keep tabs on her."

I press. "When she's here, what days is she here?"

Moe blinks. "Late usually—and Wednesday and Saturday." He pauses. "I'd stay away from her if I were you. Dolby isn't one to mess with."

I chug the rest of the gin. It was bad even for a bad joint, which this wasn't. "Thanks. I'll keep that in mind." I point to the empty glass. Moe fills it with the clear liquid. I take my glass of water and find a seat as far away from the band as possible. I like music. This isn't it. The place is filled with couples looking to hook up and guys that look like they have lost everything and everyone. I feel good that I'm not one of them. My focus is to find the man with the ring if he makes an appearance. The smoke is thick; the forced laughter thicker. Bad company and bad gin will do that to a person and place. I stare down at my glass. I don't feel drunk. I hadn't gotten drunk last night. That I was now sure of.

Then she walks in. I'm wrong. She slides in. Her step is effortless despite the floor length dress she wears. It's red like her hair and as tight as a noose on a dying man's neck. She didn't look this good last night. I take in her presence the way I had the gin–I gulped. Her eyes meet mine and widen. She hesitates, then smiles as she makes her way to my table. The music seems to fade into the background.

"Well, hello." Her voice has a lilt. I drink in the singsong the way I had the previous night. "You're back again." She pauses half a beat."I didn't think you'd be back."

"Why's that?" I try to act suave, but come off nervous.

"Buy a lady a drink?" She pulls a thin cigarette out of a silver case from the purse that hangs by her side. Her red lips wrap around the stick. I fumble in my pocket for the box of matches. I light one and then her cigarette. She inhales. She exhales a cloud of smoke up toward the ceiling. Her breathing takes mine away."What about a drink?" Flustered, I signal to Moe, who grimaces then nods.

"Why didn't you think I'd be back?" I repeat.

"You don't seem like the kind of guy who hangs out in places like this." Her eyes twinkle. They are black pools. Tar pits are black pools as well. I could die in both. "It didn't seem like you were into art."

A memory from last night prods me. "I wanted to hear more about your art."

Her eyes light up to a brighter shade of black. Her mouth forms a smile around the cigarette. "Really? Even after I told you I wasn't good?"

"Oh I'm sure you're good." I took a swig of the gin. I cough. "You wouldn't be exhibiting here if you weren't, would you?"

"It's just most people that exhibit here aren't all that famous. The Krazy Kat Klub is for the up and coming, not for the famous." Her gaze is slow as it wanders across the smoke-filled room. "I guess I'm the only one here tonight."

"You'll do." I'm light-headed, but not from the cheap booze or the smoke. "Maybe you could show me your stuff."

Her face lights up. "You'd really want that? You didn't seem very interested last night."

"Well, lets just say I had a lot to think about last night."

Tayla's expression is puzzled for a moment, then clears. "It's hard being good—at art I mean. No one takes you seriously. Even Goody just puts up with me."

"Goody?"

"Goodwin Dolby. He likes me to call him Goody. He's my patron."

"Congressman Dolby is your patron?"

She nods, her red hair bouncing against her bare shoulders. There are freckles. "He's the one who suggested I show here. He says that with the right exposure I can be a famous painter." Her smile warms my soul. Too bad it wasn't directed at me.

A ruckus in the back room draws my attention. I hear Moe yelling. It stops as he returns from the back room and slams the door shut behind him. His face is red and his mouth a thin line. He stares back at me, glaring. I ignore him and turn my attention back to Tayla. "I'm sorry, you were saying?"

"He says he can make me a big artist. Even as big as some of the dead ones." I don't respond. All the paintings on display in the Krazy Kat Klub were there for a reason. The art drew customers. Customers bought booze. "Then I can move to New York where the real art is." The band takes a break; the silence is a nice change. The small dance floor is empty and what few customers the joint has are busy either drinking or ogling each other. "Do you want to see it?"

"See what?"

"My paintings, silly."

"Sure." I'm not much on art despite having written a story or two. She takes my hand in hers across the table as we stand. Moe is staring at us, but quickly looks away when he meets my gaze. He busies himself wiping down the bar. Tayla pulls me along after her to a corner of the room where a group of small paintings hang.

"These are mine." The red-headed woman stands with a large smile in front of the display. "What do you think? Do you like them?"

I peer at the grouping. They are all landscapes done in watercolor. My eyes grow wide. "These are good. Really." I'm surprised. They aren't museum quality but they might sell.

"Really?" She beams a smile at me.

"Yes. You should try selling some of these. I'd buy one."

Her smile collapses into a frown. "Goody says he doesn't want me selling any of my things. He says I should wait until I'm famous. He says that's the best way to make money but I could really use the cash now."

I shake my head. "You should get the money while you can. Money is hard to come by nowadays."

"You think so? I wish I could. Goody wouldn't be happy."

"And you want to make Goody happy?"

"Oh yes! He's important. He has connections."

"And he has money…"

She nods. "I know! Even though I can't sell you one of my paintings, I can give you one. I'm sure Goody wouldn't mind. Which one do you want?"

I stammer, then shake my head. "I couldn't."

She eyes me a moment, then turns to the wall. She pulls a dark green and brown landscape covered with pine trees off the wall and hands it to me. I stare down at it and note the river in the background. My mind snaps back to the events of last night. I mumble a thank you. "Let's go sit down. I want to ask you a few questions. The least I can do is repay you by featuring you in the story I'm writing." We make our way back to our table. Moe grimaces when he sees me with the small canvas in my hand.

"So, tell me. Where are you from? What got you started in painting?" I have a job to do, but what I really want to know is who dumped me in the river and why. The painting pulled me back to reality.

Tayla dives into her story, taking occasional breaths to puff on a cigarette. She was born in Maryland and dropped out of high school to take care of her mother. She had come to D.C. after her mother's death. She had wanted to get a job waitressing, but the economy had turned sour in '17. She made do with odd jobs and scraped by. A year ago she ran into Congressman Goodwin Dolby who she had fallen in love with. "I still am, I think. He's nice to me and even pays the rent on my apartment." Goodwin sounded like he was getting something on the side. But I kept my mouth shut. Instead, I scribbled some notes in the notebook I carried. "So that's my life up to now. Are you going to put it all in the paper?"

"Just the artsy bits. I'm sure it will be a hit." I don't lie. At least the little old ladies that read fluff columns will like it. I doubt any serious artists read my column. Too bad. She had talent beyond her looks. The band comes back and starts playing an upbeat rendition of "Yes Sir! That's My Baby." A dark-skinned couple gets on the dance floor and attempt to Charleston to it.

"Maybe Goody will let me sell some if he sees the article and thinks it's good." Her eyes shine as she takes another puff of the cigarette. She stubs it out in the full ashtray and dives into her purse for another. She curses like a sailor then glanced up at me."You don't have one do you?"

I shake my head."Sorry. I don't smoke."

"Too bad. Give me a sec. I'll just bum one from Moe." She walks over to the bar. I scan the room, trying to see if any of the men wore the ring I had glimpsed. A few wore bands. A couple had college rings. Most wore nothing or hid what they wore. I see Tayla and Moe argue but the music makes it impossible to hear what the problem is. Tayla returns to the table flustered.

"What was that all about?"

She strikes a match and lights the new cigarette. She exhales. I watch, my senses tingling in her presence. She continues, "The jerk. He thinks he owns me."

"Does he?"

"Of course not. Everyone knows I don't like him."

I change topics. "So tell me. What happened last night?"

Her eyes blink, then stare into mine. "What do you mean?"

"You know what I mean. I was talking to you and the next thing I know I wake up in the river with a headache I'm still feeling."

She inhales sharply. This time the cigarette is between her fingers in the ashtray. "I don't know anything about that."

"Cut the crap. Who was it?" Her eyes dart the way a scared rabbit lined up in the sights of a shotgun might.

"I don't know. I told you." She didn't make it sound certain. She gets up to leave. I pull her back to her seat by her wrist. "You're hurting me."

"Sorry." I let go. "I just want to get to the bottom of whatever I fell into—and I don't mean the river. Come clean."

"I can't. I really don't know. Whatever it was, I–I don't want to be involved."

"What are you afraid of?" She bites her lip. "Tell me."

She shakes her head. Her hair flows in waves about her face. "Not here." Her voice drops to a whisper. I struggle to hear it under the music."I really don't know. ." She pulls a piece of paper and a stub of a pencil from her purse. She scribbles a moment, shoves the note across the table, then walks out of the club.

3

I walk out into the alley a few minutes later and stick around for a while hoping to spot someone with the ring on their way out. The rain stops but the night is still overcast as I walk, stepping over the puddles. The flickering light of the Krazy Kat Klub sends shards of yellowish-white reflecting off the water as I glance back. The alley is empty. I pull the collar of my raincoat up, knowing the night will be chilly after the rain. I stare down at my feet as I walk, deep in thought. I still have no clue who had tried to kill me or why. I'm sure whatever it was, was somehow related to the art in the club. Maybe it's fake or hot. I don't know, but I'd have to find out.

I turn the corner and stop. The echo of my footsteps stop. I hold my breath. A shadow turns the corner. I lunge, throwing the person onto his back with a loud "Oof". He recovers quickly, rolling on top of me. I swing and connect with the side of his head. The man yowls in pain and brings his knee up into my groin. I double up. My vision turns red. My hearing blares with a sound that resolves into a patrol car siren. As I pass out, I see the stranger scurry down the street.

I wake up where I had dropped. I'm drenched again. I have to stop waking up in water. I stagger to my feet and glance around. But whoever had followed me is long gone. The passing patrol car had frightened him off and had probably saved my life. I cough. The pain lingers, but it's tolerable and would pass. Whoever wanted me dead didn't quit. I'd been reckless. I'd have to be more careful.

I walk back to my room in the cobblestone and drop onto the bed. I let sleep take me.

4

The next morning, I decide to pay a visit to the local police precinct. Going it solo had been a mistake.

The sleepy-eyed desk Seargent looks up from the puzzle he's doing in the daily paper. "Can I help you?"

"Someone tried to kill me—twice."

He yawns."Yeah. Yeah. Who?"

"I don't know."

"Listen, bud, unless you have proof or provide a body we can't do anything. Otherwise it's just your word."

"What's your name?" I wasn't getting anywhere.

"Davis. Seargent Davis."

"Seargent, if I die I'll remember to bring my body to you."

The Seargent smirks, then says. "Ok. Calm down. So why do you think someone is trying to kill you?" I spend the next several minutes recounting the events of the last two nights. He pushes his cap back and says, "If you ask me, it sounds more like you got sloshed and passed out. What do you want me to do about it? Listen, if you had any real proof or witnesses we could help you, but as things stand you've got zip."

I hadn't thought things through. I believed if I reported the incidents to the police, they would take care of everything. It didn't work that way–at least for someone like me.

5

I returned to my place, had lunch, and cursed the world I lived in. I sat on the edge of my bed, thinking. I'm tired and sore. What I need is proof or witnesses. Well, I know one witness I just had to get her to talk. I dig through my pockets and pull out two slips of paper, and then make a call. A short time later I'm in the back of Cam's yellow on the way to Tayla's apartment. I look at Cam's toothpick in the cab's mirror. "So you interested in making an extra couple of bucks?", I ask.

The pick flicks to the other side of the cabbie's mouth. "Sure. Who do you want me to kill?" He chortles.

"Nothing like that. I just want you to tail a dame. I'll be in her place for maybe half an hour. After I leave you, hang outside. I'm betting she'll go somewhere. I want you to find out where. Then meet me outside the Krazy Kat Klub at 8 tomorrow night and let me know."

"No problem. You expectin' trouble?"

I think a long moment. "Maybe. But you should be OK. It's me they're after."

"Sure you don't want me to keep an eye on you instead? Just in case? I used to do a bit of boxing in my day." Cam slaps his chest for emphasis.

"No. I'll be OK. Just find out where she goes and let me know tomorrow." I glance out the window into the darkness. It feels like it's been raining for weeks.

Cam announces, "Here it is. This is the place." The cab slides to the curb and I hop out. I lean on the driver's door. Cam rolls the down the driver's side window.

"Try not to let her know you're following her, will you? I don't want to scare her off," I say.

"Got it, boss. Are you packing?"

I shook my head. "I don't believe in guns."

"Sure? I have one in the glove compartment. You never know when it might come in handy in my line of work. You can borrow it."

"No thanks. I'm fine. See you tomorrow." I wave and head up the steps of the small building. The cab pulls a u-turn and parks on the other side of the street. I scan the list of names posted by the door and press the buzzer that corresponds to the one that reads "Tayla Bourke". A moment later the door unlocks, and I let myself in.

6

"Come in," she calls in response to my knock on her door. I enter to find her reclining on the type of lounge I'd only seen in moving pictures. Her arm is cast nonchalantly over the rest. Her other hand holds a lit cigarette. Smoke curls toward the ceiling. She wears a blue gossamer number that tempts the viewer without revealing too much. The rest of the room is furnished in a lifestyle I know I could never attain. I know she can't either. Hanging with "Goody" Dolby had its perks

"I'm glad you came," she breathes."Don't stand there gawking and come sit by me." She pats a spot next to her. "I was hoping we could get to know each other better."

"Thanks. I prefer to stand. Did Congressman Dolby spring for this place?""Aww, don't be that way. Have a seat. Take a load off." She pauses. "Or are you afraid of me?" She smiles and my knees go weak. Thoughts of spiders pop into my mind. "Want a drink?" She pours two glasses from a carafe on a side table next to the chaise. She holds the glass out by the stem. I decide I could use a drink. I take the glass of wine and sit on the edge of the chair when I realize there is nowhere else to sit in the room. The rug is deep red and plush. The heavy drapes that cascade from the one floor-to-ceiling window match the rug. A kitchenette is off to the right; neat, clean, and doesn't look like used a lot. A single door leads to what I assume is the bedroom. A writing desk stands in one corner. Another corner serves as her painting studio. An easel, a small table, and stool hold her palette, brushes, and paints. A half-finished painting sits on the easel. I shift, my nerves jittery, on the edge of my seat."Relax," Tayla purrs as her hand moves to my arm.

"Is that your current work?" I ask, using the question as an excuse to move my arm to point. Focusing is difficult. I have to learn who had dumped me for dead.

Her glance goes to the easel. Her voice turns firm at my distraction. "Yes. It's nothing. Just a portrait I'm trying." She goes back to being seductive. "Now tell me about you. Are you married? Have a girlfriend?"

I shake my head and raise my hand to show no ring on my hand. "I wanted to ask you, I'm looking for a guy who wears a ring. A flat-faced silver ring. I think he's the guy who crowned me and dumped me in the river." Tayla's body stiffens. I continue, "You said you wanted to tell me something when we were in the club."

"I don't have anything to tell you." Her words are fast and clipped. "I—I just wanted to get to know you better." I sense it's a lie. Everything about her says she's afraid.

I stand up and face her. "Cut the game. You and I know you were there when I got clobbered. What'd you do? Spike my drink?"

Her eyes grow wide. "No, or course not. I wasn't even there." My expression must have told her I didn't believe her. "I went to powder my nose and when I got back, you were gone. I thought you had run out on me."

I wasn't sure if she was telling the truth. I had been so woozy I could have forgotten she had left the table. Right now, the only clue I have is the ring. "What about the ring? Know anyone that has one?" She shakes her head. "So who drugged me?"

"How should I know?" She lays back on the chaise. "I didn't even know you were thrown into the river until you told me." She stretches the way a cat might. "Really, I'm not lying. I just don't want to get involved." She pauses. "You should relax. You look stressed."

I walk over to the easel. I peer at the penciled sketch with dabs of color. I can't tell who it is. "Who is it?"

"No one you know."

"So were you paid to put a mickey in my drink?"

She sits up straight, then leans back."No. Don't be silly. Of course not."

"You're a bad liar."

"I'm telling the truth. I didn't see who did it."

I nod. "But you know who did." I move to the door. "Thanks for the drink."

"Don't leave. I don't want to be alone." She sits there pouting. I'm tempted, but know if I stay I'd regret it.

"Sorry, doll. I have a story deadline to meet." I want to regret it.

7

"Boss, sorry I couldn't park closer. The alley is too narrow for the cab."
It's the following evening and I'm back in Cam's cab.

"This is fine. It's probably better they don't see you.""Who?"

"Whoever's after me. What did you find out? Did you follow her?"

"Better. She hailed me about fifteen minutes after you left. I drove
her there." The toothpick shifts. "She's a real doll. You two have a
thing going?"

"No. Where did she go?"

"She was all tense and must've smoked a pack on the way. I
couldn't get a word out of her, apart from the address. The dame had
things on her mind."

I nod."So where did you take her?"

"Oh that. A big place on O Street. A real big place. I've never been in
that part of town. It's definitely out of my league, if you know what I
mean."

"O Street? I wonder who lives there."

Cam grins at me in the rear-view mirror. "I did some nosing around
after I dropped her off. I hit it off with a newsie a couple of streets
down. He says some Congressman lives in the joint. I think he said
Derby was his name."

"Dolby?"

"Yeah. That's it. He said Congressman Dolby lives there."

I give Cam a pat on his shoulder. "Good job. Listen. Can you swing
back here again around midnight? I might need a ride home later
tonight."

"Sure. You have a plan?"

"Yeah, I'm going to stir a hornet's nest."

.

8

The club is hopping. It's Saturday night and the residents of the area are out for a good time despite the economy. I'm let in by the guy at the entrance after a growl and a thorough search. He wears a simple wedding band on his ring finger. I made sure to look this time. I make my way to the bar across the crowded dance floor and as I do, I hear Moe's voice yelling in the back room. A few moments later he appears, spots me and quickly hides his surprise. "What can I do you for? Here for more info on the artists?" He indicates a table with a tilt of his head. "Most of them are here tonight. It's the big show."

I glance over. Three couples sit around a table. All are dressed to the nines and all are laughing raucously at some joke, or maybe because of the bad gin. I turn my attention back to Moe. "So what was all the yelling about?"

"Nothin'." He busies himself wiping glasses with a towel. "Just a dispute with my distributor. Nothing you have to worry about."

I nod and get right to the point. "You were here the night I got dragged out and dumped in the river." It was a statement, not a question.

"No, really? Sorry to hear." He wipes faster."Who would do such a thing?"

"Yeah. Really. So own up. Who spiked my drink and carried me out of here?"

Moe shrugs. "How should I know? I was busy tendin' bar. Besides, it's none of my business what the clientele does here—as long as it's legal, I run a straight establishment if you know what I mean."

"Like serving hooch that you pass off as gin."

He eyes me."You a Fed?"

"No. I told you. I'm a reporter."

"Yeah, yeah. Doing an art story. So you said." He looks up from the glass in his hand, his gaze locks onto mine. "Well, if you're not a Fed, I'd mind my own business if I were you."

"That a threat?"

His focus returns to the glass he is wiping. He shrugs. "Take it whatever way you want. People who look for trouble usually end up finding it."

"I'll remember that. You married? Got a college ring?"

Moe glances up at me. His expression is perplexed at the change in topic. "Nah. I don't want no dame tying me down. I finished high school. I'm student of hard knocks. Why?"

"Just trying to be friendly." He wasn't wearing a ring or had taken it off to wash the glassware. I glance around the smoke-filled room. "So where's Tayla? I don't see her tonight."

The wiping hands stop for a moment, then resume their cleaning. "She's not here."

"I can see that. Where is she?"

"Dunno. Home probably. She called in saying she was feeling sick and wouldn't make the party."

"Too bad."

"So you going to order something or just waste my time flappin' your jaw?"

"I'll take a shot of the best water you have."

"It's all the same. It's not like we have much choice nowadays." He pours a small glass and places it in front of me. I drop my loose change on the bar and include a tip. He scoops the money. "Thanks."

"So I hear Congressman Dolby hangs out here on occasion."

"Then you heard wrong."

"Oh? I could have sworn someone told me he was the patron of this place."

"You heard wrong. He's the patron of the art show, but he doesn't patronize the place. Remember what I told you about sticking your nose into things that aren't your business." His hand comes up from under the bar. It's holding a large steak knife.

I raise my hands. "Hey, I didn't mean anything by it. I was just hoping to talk to him about the show." Moe relaxes and puts the knife back where it had come from.

"Maybe you should check at the Capitol. He doesn't hang out here.

He's never been here. Get it?"

"Sure. I got it." I got that Congressman Goodwin Dolby not only hung out there but didn't want people knowing he hung out there. It was one thing to be an art patron. It was another to be associated with a speakeasy, especially if you were a government employee. But it wasn't any of my concern. What I wanted was the man with the ring. He held all the answers.

9

The band went on break and the dancing couples retired to their respective tables and booths. The table of artists is even louder now that the music has stopped. I make my way to them. They pause their celebration to look up at the man who had interrupted their revelry.

"My name is Randy Cook and I write for the Washington Court Herald. I was wondering if I could interview you about the art show and your art. "Their interest is piqued. I lied, "I was most impressed by it all. "Their interest rises, and I am soon sitting at the table with them. After a round on me, I had all the information I needed. They were all would-be artists trying to make it big in D.C. They had all been approached by Congressman Dolby, who they said had taken them under his wing to promote their work. Of course they had jumped at the chance. And of course, none of them merited a fully furnished and paid apartment the way Tayla had. None of them had her curves. I scanned their hands. Those who had rings wore bands. One man had a white stripe where a ring would be. I figured he'd be hiding a wedding ring, not the type of ring I was looking for. I had struck out. I tried a different approach. "So Congressman Dolby is a patron to you all. Does he come here often? "

One man with thick round glasses wheezed, then spoke. "Yes. Such a wonderful person. "His speech slurred. He put his finger up to his lips. "Shh. He wants to keep it secret. Says he doesn't want the fame or glory. Good man, that. "

"So, how much does he pay you? That's what a patron does, right? "

The man's eyebrows shoot up. "Dear lad, no. We paid him. It's an investment in our future, he says. "

"You paid him? For what? "

He spreads his hands wide. "Why for setting up this art exhibit, of course. It costs money to host something like this. "

"So when is he going to pay you? "

The man blinks. "When our art is appreciated by the critics and community, of course. "

So, "Goody" Dolby had a scam going, and these lunkheads didn't see it for the glory and booze. A balding man next to a crinkly old woman says, "He's swell. He said we all had great potential. We just needed a place where people can see your work. "

"How much did you pay him? "

The man blinks behind the glasses. "Fifty bucks. I know I can make that back in no time once people see my work. Hey, you got a photographer? You can take pictures and put them in the paper along with your story. "

I shake my head. There's a sucker born every minute and I've stumbled on four minutes' worth. "No. Sorry. It's just a text piece. I'm sure I'll do a good job describing your work. "

"You better. "A lean drink of a man chortles. "If we don't get good press, we'll know who wrote it. "I had all I needed. I feign spotting a friend and quickly excuse myself from the clutch of artists.

10

I wander over to the band that is still on break smoking butts and sipping drinks.

"How's tricks? " I offer a light to the drummer who is a sullen man who looked like he was born that day. No ring on him.

"Thanks. Ok. Hey, didn't I see you the other night talking to a dame, real hot number? "

I nod. "You didn't happen to see what happened when I left that night, did you? "

Sullen shakes his head. "No. We went out for some air and when we got back you and the broad was gone. Why? "

"Oh, nothing. I was just wondering if you kew where she went. " I lied because I figured there was no sense in having too many people ask questions about my questions. "So you guys regulars here? " A nod. "I hope Moe pays you guys enough. You're good. " I was fishing and he took the nibble.

"Yeah the pay's decent for this town. Nothing to write home about though. "

"Times are tough all over. Glad Moe runs an upright joint. I've been in places where the owner's a scum. "

The drummer shakes his head. "Oh, he's not the owner. "

"No? "

"No. Funny thing that. He gives us our cash, regular like. But he always goes in the back room and has it out with the boss-man first. He's never happy doling out the cash, I guess. "

Bingo. "So who's the boss if he isn't? "

A shrug. "Dunno. Never seen him. I hear he likes to keep it quiet and low. I figger he has a rap and is trying to keep it on the hush side. Listen, thanks for the light. It's time for the last set. "

11

I nod and make my way around the room as the band starts a slow song I don't recognize. A few couples get up and move to the dance floor. I survey the paintings on the walls since I figure I should at least give the foursome a shot. I recognize the names from the group at the table, others I haven't run into. I pause at Tayla's corner. She's the best of them and I wonder if Goodwin charged her before he sponsored her. Somehow, I doubt it. He was running a scam that I was sure of, but he got lucky with her. She was good, too good for a place like this.

Yelling from the back room pulls my attention from her landscapes."I've told you bums not to deliver the stuff when we're open. How much simpler can I put it?" Moe's glance darts between the argument and the crowd. His voice drops to a level below the noise, and I can't make out the rest of the argument. The band and crowd are making too much noise and having too much fun to notice the ruckus. I go back to the bar. Moe glares when he sees me.

"What do you want?"

"I just want a refill." My tone is as innocent as I can make it. With a grunt he reaches under the bar and pulls up a bottle. It's empty."One second. I need to get a few fresh ones." Moe pulls several empties out and scurries into the back room. I strain to see into the room, but the door swings shut automatically behind him. I see the door isn't locked. A minute later Moe returns, his arms laden with bottles which he places behind the bar. "I hope it's the good stuff."

He shoots lightning bolts from his eyes. "If you don't like it, complain to the Feds. Do you want it or not?"

"Fill 'er up!" I toss an extra buck on the counter to smooth his ruffled feathers. He grunts but his disposition doesn't improve. "So when is Tayla going to be back?" The lightning now has dark clouds.

He shrugs. "How should I know? It's not like she's mine." I toss an extra sawbuck on the bar. He picks it up. "What's this for?"

"You know the ring I asked about?"

"Yeah." He eyes me with suspicion.

"That's for letting me know if you see anyone in here wearing one." He pockets the bill.

"Sure."

I wasn't sure, but I figured it was a worthwhile investment. If he could finger the guy who had dumped me, it was worth it. Besides, maybe I had a story and I could expense it. If it didn't pan out, I was out a fiver.

12

I need fresh air and I want to check out the rear of the club to see if there is a way into the back room, so I wander out into the night and make my way behind the building. I figure whoever was in the back room had to have a back entrance, especially if he was yelling about deliveries. I'm right. Not only is there a back way in, but there is a small courtyard set up with a couple of chairs and a table. The courtyard is off a small side street used for deliveries and not on the alley where the main entrance is. The courtyard would be a romantic spot if wasn't raining. A shaft of yellow light streams through the rain from a curtained window. I step closer and peer in. The drapes are too thick, the slit too thin. The window is barred. Whoever's inside likes their privacy. I don't bother testing the door. I'm certain it's locked. I stop. Something feels wrong. I take a moment to realize the rain doesn't sound right, hitting the cobblestones of the courtyard. I look up and spot a shadow in the branches of a large oak. Puzzled, I stand staring as the rain splatters across my face. Then I have it. It's a treehouse. Who would have thought there would be a treehouse in the middle of D.C. ? Why would a club have a treehouse? I'd have to check it out during the daylight. Right now, the rain comes down in buckets. I pull my collar up and go back in past the bouncer who stands drenched under the overhang. He gives me the once over, recognizes me, glares at me, and nods, which tells me I can go in without another pat down. The security is shoddy.

The smoke, laughter, and noise hit me like a wall. Moe is talking to one of the customers. From her stance she is having none of it. The artists are on the dance floor stumbling around in their attempt at dancing. The men are grappling with the women more than actually dancing. The women laugh and push them away just when it looks like they would be caught. I decide it's time to upset the hornets. I walk up to the door to the back room and tug on the knob. It's locked. "Hey! You're not allowed in there." Moe is quickly at my side and pulls me away from the door. I'm flung against the bar. I raise my hands in submission.

"Sorry. I just thought it was the men's room." Moe takes a step forward then stops, aware he's drawn the attention of several of the customers. He thinks better about coming at me and instead brushes me off in mock concern.

"Sorry sir. That room is private. We have no on-premises restrooms. You can use the one a few doors down at the gas station." His eyes shoot daggers at me. "Remember what I told you before." His voice drops to a low snarl, too quiet for anyone but me to hear. Moe glances at the clock behind the bar and calls out. "Last call. Get your last drinks for the night."

I walk out into the pouring rain. I'd done enough for one night. I climbed into the back of Cam's cab and fell against the seat, exhausted and shaking.

13

The sun is out the next morning, but my mood is still with the rain. Last night I thought I'd made progress. Today I realize I am no closer to finding whoever it was that dunked me. I go out to clear the cobwebs in my head. I pick up a paper from the corner stall. The headline screams the Ku Klux Klan was going to march on D.C. next week. I toss the rag back on the pile, feeling dirty. I find a copy of the Court Herald and am glad to see the headline doesn't mention the march in sensationalist terms. Instead, there is a story about the fallout from the Scopes trial and just a small mention of the Klan. A guy in a suit with an umbrella under his arm picks up the rag. I see the sparkle of a ring on his hand. I stare.

"Excuse me."

"Yes?" The fellow looks up at my interruption.

"I can't help but notice you wear your ring facing your palm. Can I ask why?" The man holds up his hand and looks at the diamond wedding ring.

He shrugs. "It's more comfortable this way. That and it doesn't draw attention from the wrong type, if you know what I mean. A lot of men do it this way." I thank him and walk back to my building. I may have seen the ring but hadn't known it. I had never worn a ring. I'd have to try the club again. I was sure Moe wouldn't be thrilled with having me back, but if I could get in, I'd try to not attract his attention. I sat down on the stoop and considered what I'd learned. Then, I got up and called Cam.

14

Once I'm back in the cab, I ask the toothpick, "So, want to make a few more extra bucks?"

"Sure. More shadow work? Where to now?"

"Now? Back to Tayla's. And no, nothing as easy as tailing someone. You'll have to walk around a bit."

"Dangerous?"

"I don't think so."

"Too bad. I was hoping to use this." He gives the glove compartment a pat.

"Don't pack. They won't let you in that way."

"What's the score?"

"I want you to go into the Krazy Kat Klub tonight. Just mingle. Buy a drink—don't get drunk. Look for any guy wearing a ring."

"Sorry, I'm not into guys. Dolls are more my style."

"Just do it OK? I don't want you to marry them. Just look for someone that wears their ring on the inside of the palm. Know what I mean?"

"Yeah, I get you. What do you want me to do with him?"

"Just get back to me and let me know who it is, and if you can figure out the kind of ring it is. Oh, and keep an eye out on the back room. If anyone goes in or out, let me know. Got it?"

"Got it."

The cab pulls up outside of Tayla's building. I hand a fiver to Cam as I say, "Oh, and be sure to dress up. It's not a dive."

15

Once I'm buzzed in, I walk up the steps and knock on Tayla's door. It opens a crack and a face peers at me. "Go away."

"I thought you wanted to be friends." My comeback isn't very suave or original. It doesn't work.

"I don't want to talk to you."

I'm taken aback when I spot a dark ring around the eye that watches me from the door. "Are you OK?"

"I'm fine. Go away?"

"What happened to your eye?"

"I—I had an accident."

"Run into a doorknob?" I feel uneasy and know something's wrong. "Sorry, that was supposed to be a joke. I just want to talk. Can I come in?"

The eye looks at me a moment then disappears as the door shuts. I hear the chain being freed. The door opens. "Come on in." I enter the room. It hasn't changed much apart from a dress tossed onto the chaise. Tayla is wearing a long fluffy bathrobe and no makeup. Apart from the shiner, she was still pretty but not ravishingly glamorous like before. "Want some coffee?" She moves to the kitchen. I follow. She pulls a pot out of a cabinet and puts some coffee into the metal pot. This wasn't the Tayla I had met at the club. This was Tayla, the person.

"No thanks. I've had mine."

"You don't mind if I do, do you? I'm still waking up. Have a seat. Sorry, I don't get much company."

"So, do you want to talk about it? The eye, I mean."

"Nothing to talk about. I told you I had an accident." Her hand shakes as she pours water from the tap into the pot. She puts it onto the burner and lights the stove. She drops into the chair across from me and knocks a cigarette out of a pack.

"Moe said you were sick."

She shrugs. "I don't want people to see me this way."

"So why did you let me?"

"I was getting lonely—and you like my art." She takes a drag from the cigarette and exhales. It's a tired exhale.

I took a guess."So Goodwin hit you?" She flinches, but recovers. The more I learn of the Congressman the more I hate him."What happened?"

"He—he hit me. He got angry. I'd never seen him that way. I told him about you and how you were writing an article about me and my art." She sobs.

"Is that why he hit you? Because of my story?"

She looks up at me through red eyes, one black. "No—he didn't care about the story. He said I shouldn't have told you about him. He—he said he told me not to mention him to anyone. He said he didn't want any publicity. He liked his privacy." Tayla bursts into tears.

"I bet." The coffee is boiling, so I get up and turn off the stove. I rummage through the cabinets and find a cup. I pour some of the black liquid into it. "Sugar or cream in your Joe?" She shakes her head. I place the cup in front of her. She picks it up in both hands and sips.

"He's always been so nice to me—and—and no one has ever hit me before."

"He's a slime. I'll call the cops on him."

Tayla looks up at me, aghast. "No. Please don't do that. I don't want to cause any more trouble."

"But he hit you."

"I'll be OK. Please don't tell the cops." I sit down next to her, unsure of what I should say or do. "Please? For me?" She forces a smile through her tears. "I—I don't want you to get hurt either."

"Ok. I promise. But if he ever hits you again, you know where you can find me. Deal?"

She nods as she takes another sip. She wipes her eyes."I bet I look a mess, don't I?"

"You look fine to me." I wasn't lying.

16

"Where to?" Cam asks the following day.

"The mansion on O Street."

"The place I dropped the doll off at?"

"Yeah. Remember where it was?"

"Sure thing, boss."

"So what happened last night?", I ask.

"Very hoity-toity place. Not my style, if you know what I mean. Too upper crust. The gin was good though."

"The ring. Did you see a guy with a ring on the inside?"

The toothpick disappears into Cam's mouth to reappear a second later. "Nope. I checked everyone inside. No inside rings." He laughs at his own joke.

I'm disappointed. I'd hoped Cam would have more luck than I had. "How about the back room? Anyone go in or out?"

"Just the bartender. I kept my eyes peeled. Did I do good?"

"Yeah. Thanks."

"Anytime you want me to do some more legwork for you, I'm all in. Provided of course you pay again." Cam chuckles as the car pulls up in front of a large stone building on O Street. "This is the place, boss. Do you want me to hang around?"

"Sure. I don't expect to be very long. If I'm not out in half an hour call the Marines."

He turns to look at me from the front seat."You serious? You expecting trouble?"

"Nah. Just trying to make a joke."

17

I stroll up the walkway to the large front door. The building is white marble and seems more like a government building than someone's home. Whoever built it hadn't spared cost. I ring the bell and a moment later a black manservant opens the door. I'd heard they had abolished slavery. Apparently, Goodwin Scriven hadn't. "I'd like to see the Congressman, please."

"The Congressman is occupied."

"Tell him I'm with the Washington DC Court Herald and I'm here to do an interview." I pull my pencil and notebook out of my pocket to enhance my words.

"One moment. I will see if the Congressman is free." I'm left standing on the porch. People this rich should have a waiting room–or maybe it's just me. Several minutes later, I'm about to give up when the servant returns. "The Congressman will see you." He leads me me through a long hall that looks like it's part of a museum. Busts of people I don't recognize adorn either side. I walk through the open door at the end of the hall into a richly furnished office. Heavy drapes hang from tall windows that are open. The breeze barely makes them stir. The room smells clean.

18

A rotund man sits behind the desk. His pallor is sallow and his hair non-existent. His bulldog of a face looks up at me as I enter. He doesn't bother to stand to greet me. His gaze scans me from head to toe. There is no expression of approval or disapproval. "What can I do for you?" His voice is a frog-like croak. "I'm a busy man." I reintroduce myself, even though I am certain his servant would have told him who I was.

I dive in. "My paper wants to do a story on the D.C. art scene and the up-and-coming painters. I was told you are sponsoring some of the artists who are on exhibit at the Krazy Kat Klub." Dolby doesn't flinch. "Is that true?"

"Why yes. In fact, I am." His voice is a croak of pride. I hadn't expected an admission after all I had heard about his desire for privacy. "I sponsored a few artists I've met that I feel are worth following and nurturing."

"Could you tell me who you think the best are and how and where you met them?" Dolby expounds on his meeting several of the people I had met the night before. When he is done, he hasn't mentioned Tayla. I brought her up. "So what do you think of Tayla Bourke?" He flinches. "I mean, as far as her art goes?"

Congressman Goodwin recovers quickly. "Her artwork? Purely amateur in my estimation."

He is lying. I don't know why. "Then why sponsor her?"

"She came and begged me to give her a chance. She said she was desperate. I decided I'd do a good deed and give her a small corner of the art exhibit. I thought she might get lucky and sell one or two pieces." He spreads his hands expansively. "It's the least I could do for someone on the down and outs." He pauses. "After all, isn't that what being a servant of the people is all about?"

"Oh, certainly. I'm glad to hear you say that." His grin is thin and forced. He clasps his hands at his chin. There is a ring, but I can't see the inside of his hands. "So have you and Mrs. Dolby been out to see the exhibit?"

The grin fades. "No. I stay away from clubs like that. It wouldn't be good for me to be seen in a gin joint, politically that is. The only reason I have the show there is they charge little, and I didn't want to gamble on the show falling through in a regular place that cost me an arm and a leg." He pauses. "I'd like to keep my involvement with the art show on the hush-hush. I'm just trying to do a good deed. I don't need my name splattered all over the pages. The only reason I'm telling you all of this is to promote the wonderful artists themselves." He rises from the chair. "Now if you excuse me, I have a lot of paperwork I need to take care of."

I reach forward and shake his hand. He hesitates, then extends his own. I'm uncertain, but the ring doesn't feel to be more than a band against my palm. Dolby wipes his hand on his pants and grimaces before he pushes a call button on the wall. The servant enters a moment later. I turn back to the Congressman. "So what do you, as the servant of the people, think about the rumors of a Klan march on Washington?" For an instant, the servant's expression breaks. "Do you think it's a disgrace in this day and age?"

Hatred is clear in Dolby's eyes. His tone is even. "There are all kinds of people in this world. It's not my role to judge, but to fulfill their wishes. Good day."

I walk down the hall to the exit. The servant follows behind. "So what do you think of the Congressman?" I ask as I step out onto the porch.

"It's not my role to judge, but between you and me, sir, I have a job." I nod and head out onto the street. I spot Cam's cab parked a block down. A minute later I'm being driven home.

19

"How'd it go?"

"Just as I suspected. The man's a monster and tries to tell a good story. It was all I could do to keep from landing one on him.

"So he the one with the ring?"

I shake my head, then see Cam isn't watching me in the mirror. "No. I'm pretty sure he's not the one. Now I'm back to square zero. At least I got some background on the art show. He's playing it like he's doing it as a favor to the artists but from where I sit it stinks scam. The guy is milking the poor saps up front, throws a one-off show to make them happy then tells them things didn't pan out for them. That's how I see it."

"So what next? You going back to the club again?"

I had run out of ideas. "Nah. I'm going to stay home and write the article. The deadline's day after tomorrow. Maybe after the article's off my mind I can think straight and figure things out."

The cab moves along a curved stretch of road just outside of D.C. We are a couple of miles from my place. The roads are wet from the previous rains and traffic is light. I'm going to tell Cam to meet me again tomorrow when a black Ford speeds up to pass us. At the last instant it swerves and with a crash of metal, the yellow rumbles off the road. Cam curses. I grab the back of his seat. Cam fights to keep the car out of the trees. A screech of rubber and the Ford races out of sight. I bounce as the cab hits the ditch by the side of the road and grinds to a halt.

Cam exhales. I see the toothpick is still between his lips. "You OK? Stupid jerk. Traffic's gotten bad lately. Everyone seems to be in a rush."

I sit, letting my breathing and racing heart slow down. I nod and gulp.

Cam turns the key. The engine sputters but doesn't start. He tries again. He curses. Another try. "I think it's flooded. I'm going to check for any damage." He opens his door and climbs out onto the muddy ground. A moment later, he kicks the door and curses again. He leans into the driver's side window. "We won't be going anywhere for a while. The tire's blown. The cab's scraped up, but not too bad. I think the Ford got the worst of it. I have a spare in the back. It'll take a while to change. Then I think I can back out onto the road." He moves to the trunk and starts work on the tire. I'm still shaking when I step out of the cab to give Cam a hand. "We were lucky. The accident could have been worse." Cam points to the large tree we had stopped short of hitting.

"I don't think it was an accident."

Cam looks up from the jack. "No? You mean they ran us off on purpose?"

"That's my bet."

"Why?"

"I guess I'm getting too close. To what, I don't know. But I have a pretty good guess who."

20

I spend the next day at home writing the article. I keep the Congressman's name out of it, because I don't want the paper in a lawsuit after he asked me not to print his connection. I just make it "an anonymous benefactor." Besides, I don't feel like he deserves accolades from what I've learned about him and how he treats those around him. I drop the story off at the office, then decide to go for a walk to clear my head and figure out what I should do until I got my next assignment. I'm pretty certain Dolby was either in the Ford that had run us off or knew who was. Tayla had told him about me, but he hadn't brought it up. He hadn't wanted me to use his name in the article, but that wasn't a reason to run us off the road, especially since the story wasn't even out. He may also have had me dumped in the river. The only common thread I could come up with was the art show, Tayla, and the Congressman were all related to the Krazy Kat Klub. That would be where I would look again.

I check my watch. It's just after 2 P. M. The club won't open until 5. I change directions and walk toward the club. Half an hour later, I stand in the courtyard. I check the back door. It's locked. I look at the window and as it had been the other night; the drapes are drawn. I move around to the main entrance. I have no hope they have left the door unlocked, but I check none the less. I'm not wrong. I stand in the alley staring at the sign about soap. I consider breaking in, but decide against it. I don't want to end up on the front page, or even the third, as a headline about breaking and entering. I make my way back to the courtyard. I spot the treehouse I had noticed before. I scratch my chin, wondering why it even existed. There didn't seem to be a way up. I walk around the base of the large tree and spot a run of twine tacked to the bark. I reach up and give the string a yank. A rope ladder drops out of the structure and hits the tree with a slap.

21

This is no kid's treehouse. There is a small table and two chairs on a rug that probably cost more than all the furniture in my apartment. A small wooden chest stands off to one side. I swing the lid open and discover a fine place setting for two and a small candelabra. This is a lover's retreat. I wonder if the Congressman availed himself of this spot. Something is off. The outside of the chest is deeper than the inside. I remove the contents and place it on the table. I knock on the wooden bottom of the chest. It sounds hollow. I press, poke, and prod. A click rewards my hunting when my finger finds a tiny button on the inside of the chest. The bottom comes free and I see a white cloth covering the contents of the chest.

I lift the cloth and gasp. I've found a Klansman's robe, and under it, the hood. I stand staring. The Congressman is a closet Klansman. I wonder how many of his constituents know. This is a bigger scandal than scamming artists. I frown. I only have circumstantial evidence the robes are his. I have to tie him directly to the Klan. I am sure the upcoming march will be an opportunity. If he is going to attend, he will need the costume. I would have to keep an eye on him and the treehouse.

22

The sound of a truck pulling up causes my heart to pound. I replace the false bottom and the contents of the chest and let the lid drop. Voices from the truck draw my attention. I peer out of the treehouse to see a red delivery truck in the street. Two burley men joke as they walk to the back door of the club. One of them knocks three times. A moment later Moe comes out. Chatting, the three of them move back to the truck. I watch, keeping a low profile, as they return carrying cases of bottles. The club is getting its gin delivery in the middle of the day–in broad daylight. Most bootleggers delivered under cover of night. This was brazen. A couple of minutes later, the three men reappear. Moe waves as the truck drives off down the street. He turns to go back into the club, then stops and stares at the treehouse.

I duck inside, terrified he'd spotted me. My heart pounds up into my throat. I hold my breath and wait to see his head pop up into the treehouse. I fall back against the chest as the rope ladder comes flying at me. I lay panting. I hear the door to the club slam shut. Terrified, I wait several minutes until I've calmed down and am certain Moe isn't coming back. I lower the ladder, scramble down, then toss it back into the treehouse the way Moe had probably done. Unnerved, I high-tail it back to my apartment.

23

I had stumbled onto something big. I knew Dolby was a scammer, hit women, and hid behind his power and hood. I wondered what his constituents would think if they found out. I also knew he didn't deserve to hold his office. Congressman Goodwin Dolby's Klan affiliation was a bigger story than his scamming artists. What he had done to Tayla was reason enough for me to finger him and see justice done. But Dolby was a racist of the worst sort. He probably wouldn't get thrown in jail, but he would be disgraced. I've discovered why there had been two attempts on my life. Now I need to find his associate, the man with the ring. That had been a dead end so far. I have to find another way so I decide to visit a local jeweler.

24

An hour later, I walk into a store. A bell cheerfully jingles over the door as it shuts. The place is tiny and cramped. The walls are filled to overflowing with cheap rings, watches, and brooches. The good stuff is in the lone glass case; a little old man stands behind it. He eyes me with suspicion–nervous and unsure. I could have gone to a fancy place in downtown D.C. but this was a couple of blocks away.

"Can I help you?" His accent is thick. Just like his glasses.

"I'm interested in a ring."

"I carry many rings." He points to a tray of rings on the wall to my left. "I'm sure you will find something suitable for your lady."

I grimace. He'd pegged me for someone who couldn't pay for the rings in the glass case. He was right. "Uh, no. I'm not looking for an engagement ring."

"Oh? How about a nice college ring? You did go to college, didn't you?" It's more of an accusation that I didn't, than a question. I'm starting to hate the guy.

"What's your name?"

"Fredrick. You can call me Fred. Everyone does."

"Well Fred, I'm looking for a very specific, special ring."

"Special rings cost money."

Flustered, I stammer, then continue. "No. You don't get it. I don't want to buy."

"Then the door is behind you."

"Look! I want information."

"Ah. Information. Why didn't you say so?"

I grumble to myself about not having had a chance. "I'm trying to find a ring. It's silver. It's like a signet ring but flat and without a signet." Fred looks puzzled, his expression blank. I continue, "You do know what a signet ring is, don't you?"

"Yes, of course. I am a jeweler. It is my business to know."

"Well? Do you know what I'm talking about?"

"Why would someone buy a signet ring without a signet?"

"No. You don't get me. The guy I'm looking for has a ring. It's not a signet ring. It's like a signet ring. It's like a band, but has a flat disk of silver instead of a signet. Get it? Instead of a raised part it has a like— like a tiny silver mirror."

The jeweler stares at me for a moment. "Ah! I understand."

"Well?"

He shakes his head. "I know of such rings but I do not sell or am able to."

"I told you, I don't want to buy. I just want to find the man who has one."

"There are many, from what I hear."

"In the D.C. area?"

"More than in any other. It is a government ring. That is why I cannot sell it."

"Government ring? What do you mean?"

The small man shrugs. "All I know is people in the government wear it."

"What part of the government?"

"I cannot say. I have never seen such a ring, but I have heard stories."

"What stories?"

"That it is a government ring."

What the Hell is a government ring? So whoever had taken me for a swim had worked for the government? That made sense in a strange way. If my assailant worked for the government, they were probably associated with Congressman Dolby. The pieces were falling into place, but I had no clue what the picture was. I thank Fred, promise I'd buy an engagement ring at the discount he offered me if I ever decided I was desperate enough to need one, and then leave the small shop, the bell jingling cheerfully behind me.

25

I sit down at my tiny kitchen table—more like a card table, with a hot cup of Joe. I am no closer to finding my assailant, but I have one more clue. It feels important because of its possible connection to Dolby. I pick up the phone and call Cam. A half hour later, I'm in the back of the cab.

"Where to, Boss?"

"Back to Tayla's."

"You really got a thing for her, don't you?"

"I just want to make sure she's OK. She's had it rough."

"If you say so." The cabbie's eyes fix on me in the rear-view. I ignore him.

"What's the date today?"

"Dame, calendar, or fruit?" Cam guffaws. "Why?"

"Calendar." Cam tells me. It's a few days before the planned march on D.C. As to the why I want to know, I explain it to him. The toothpick jumps from side to side.

"I never got the point of those guys. It's 1925 for chris-sake. You'd think those guys would wise up and get with the times."

"I guess some people can't get rid of the past because they have no future." The cabbie grunts. I continue, "Listen, I want you to do something important. I want you to hang out at the club—out back. There's a treehouse..." Cam's eyebrows raise in the mirror. "I want you to stake it out and let me know who goes in it. OK?"

"Sure, boss. As long as I get paid. I have to make money to survive, you know. Unless there's gunplay." He taps the glove compartment. "Then it's on the house. So you think whoever took you for a swim is using this treehouse?"

"No. Yes. Maybe. I don't know. There's something going on and I'm trying to find out what. Just watch. Don't do anything stupid."

"You can count on me. I'm not the hero type. So what do you think is going on?"

"I'll tell you when I have all the facts. Hey, have you ever heard of a government ring?"

"Like a ring of thieves? They all are, if you ask me." Cam glances up at me in the mirror.

"No, like the ring I was looking for. I found out it might be a ring worn by those in government."

"No." The back of his head shakes in the seat in front of me. "So the guy you're looking for works for the government? Like a Fed or G-Man?"

"That's what I'm trying to find out."

"Well, here you are." The cab pulls up in front of Tayla's building.

26

"I don't want you seeing Dolby," I tell Tayla. Her black eye has turned a tinge of green, a sure sign it's healing. "He's a dangerous man. I don't want you hurt."

She looks at me across the kitchen. She's sipping a cup of coffee by the stove. "You really care, don't you?" Her smile is genuine and warm enough it could melt the ice in the icebox. "I thought you were just digging for dirt on the art show."

I flinch. "At first I was. I had a story to do. The story went to press. Then I saw what he'd done to you. I want you to promise me you won't see him again."

"But what about my paintings? I can't just leave them at the club."

I had forgotten about them. "Will he be there?"

"I don't know. But Moe has strict orders not to sell or let the paintings out of the building without his say so."

"How long is the exhibit going to stay up? Didn't you tell me the other day through this weekend?" Tayla nods. "Well, they'll be safe where they are for the time being. We'll figure something out this weekend. Until then, keep out of Dolby's reach. Ok?" Another nod. "I'm not sure what's going on, but the Congressman deals dirty. He's been scamming artists and taking their money to promote them. Did you pay him anything?" I don't mention the Klan.

She blinks those beautiful eyes. "Yes. He said he wanted the money to help set up the exhibit. I pay him every month."

I glance around the ritzy apartment. At least she was getting the better end of the deal. I didn't want to ask, but I had to know. "Did he set you up in this place?"

"He said artists had to have nice things or people wouldn't take them seriously. He also said it was close to his place."

"Are—are you his girlfriend? Did you know he was married?" I thought I knew the answer, but I wanted to hear it straight from her. Tayla says nothing. The blood drains from her face. "Come clean. I want to know."

"No. I didn't know. I—I'm not that kind of girl. I thought we had a thing going. Really, I didn't know he was married. The dirtbag! Believe me!"

"I believe you. He used you."

"The jerk! I don't want to have anything to do with him. I thought he was a perfect gentleman until he hit me." Her voice breaks. "I was a fool! A complete fool! How could I have been so stupid to think he liked me?" She looks around the apartment. "I can't stay here knowing what I do. What am I going to do? Where am I going to stay? I—I can't afford a place like this on my own. All of this stuff belongs to him." She breaks down in tears, collapsing into my arms.

"It's not your fault. He's slime. I'm going to do all I can to make him pay. You're a good kid. She looks up at me through tear-filled eyes. I kiss her. She melts in my arms.

27

The next night I'm back at the Krazy Kat Klub. Cam had reported that no one had come near the treehouse, even though there had been a couple making out in the courtyard. It's raining again, a cold rain, as I walk up to the entrance. The bouncer eyes me and pats me down. I decide to see if he could shed some light on the Congressman's involvement."How's it going?"

"Ok." He wasn't the talkative type.

"Busy?"

"Nah."

"You don't talk much." He grunts. I took my shot. "Have you seen Congressman Dolby come in tonight?"

"What's it to ya?"

"I'm just making small talk. You must get bored standing here while everyone is having a good time inside."

"You going to go in or stand here exercising your jaw?"

I shrug. I was getting nowhere. I go in and head to the bar. As I expected, Moe is there. He's the only one who worked there apart from the bouncer and the man in the back, who I figured was Dolby.

"How's it going tonight?"

Moe looks up at me. "You again?"

"I'll have the usual." I think I'm being funny. Moe just curls his lip in a snarl and pours a glass of what passes for booze in this place.

"I notice you have a treehouse out back." Moe grunts an acknowledgment. "What's it for? I didn't think a gin joint needed one."

"We ain't a gin joint. We're a social club that promotes art." His response is well-rehearsed. I grunt in turn. He continues more casually, "it's for weddings and such. You know, a cozy nook for the happy couple, if you know what I mean."

"You get a lot of those, do you?"

"Not that many. A few. It's a classy time when we do."

I nod. "Who's idea was it? It seems like it would draw people." I down the gin, clench my teeth, and point at the empty glass.

"The boss."

"Who's that? I thought you were the boss," I lie.

"No one you know." Moe fills my glass. "I just run the bar."

"I'd love to meet him." I play with the glass. "Anyone that can set up a place like this in the middle of D.C. must have some smarts."

"Yeah. I'd stop nosing around, if I were you."

Moe isn't revealing anything. I try another approach. "So you get a lot of government types here—being in D.C. and all?"

"I wouldn't know. It's not like we check their I.D. As long as they pay cash and don't cause problems anyone is welcome."

"Even the Klan?"

He looks puzzled, then shrugs. "As long as they don't wear their outfits and don't hassle the regulars. We serve all colors here."

I nod. "I noticed. I guess you didn't hear they're planning a march on D.C. this weekend?"

He is surprised. "Nah. I don't read the rags." I don't take it personally since I don't work for a rag.

"No one here is part of the Klan, are they?" I didn't expect a yes for an answer.

"Not that I know of. Why?"

"Just wondering. I was thinking maybe I could do an interview for the Herald. You know, a human interest story."

"Well, I hope they stay away from here. I have to serve everyone but I'd rather not serve their kind." He pauses. "I'd think you'd want to stay away from them too." There is a longer pause. "I hear Tayla's not coming back."

"Oh?" There was no reason to advertise what was going on between Tayla and me.

"Yeah. Seems she's still sick. I hope it's nothing serious."

"Yeah. She seemed nice."

"You wouldn't know anything about what happened, would you?"

"No. Why should I?"

He shrugs. "I don't know. You two seemed chummy the other night."

"Sorry. Don't have a clue."

Moe looks at me askance. A dowdy woman dressed in black and pearls walks up and orders a "water". She looks at me in a way that says she wants to know me better. I beat it. The room isn't as full as the night of the party, but it's still full of smoke and laughter. I spot one of the four artists I'd met the other night. He sits alone in a corner. I saunter over and say, "Mind if I join you?" He looks up at me puzzled, then recognition hits.

28

"You're the reporter, right?" His speech slurs. "Sit down. Sit down."

"You seem to be celebrating."

"Celebrating? Nah! It's a wake."

"A wake? For who?"

"Me. I'm dead. Can't you tell?"

"How so?"

"I—I'm broke. Ju—just spent the last of my money on this most excellent alco—holic beverage. I haven't sold a single picture. Mr. Dolby said I was good, but no one bought anything. Phi—philistines, all of them."

I figure it's better I don't voice my opinion of his art. Instead, I say, "I wrote about you and your art. The story should be out tomorrow. Maybe that will help."

"You, sir, are a gentleman. But now Mr. Dolby wants another down payment on the space. I—I can't afford it. I cannot pay. This show was my last hope." His vision firms. "It's all his fault. He said he'd make me famous. He said I was good. I'll kill him." His shoulders and face droop. "No. He's not worth the effort. I should pack up and move back down to Atlanta. I'm sure my folks would take me back." His face falls onto the table with a thud. I check his hands and find no ring.

I decide I won't be getting anything more from him. I make the rounds and observe the hands of everyone I can for the mysterious ring. An hour later, I decide I've had enough and make my way outside. I stand a moment by the entrance, filling my lungs with the night. The rain has stopped, and the air smells clean. The guy who takes care of security leans against the wall, eyeing me.

"You going back in?"

"No. I'm done for tonight. What's your name, by the way?"

"Jericho Waldroup. Why?"

"I'm just trying to be friendly. I see you here whenever I visit."

"I don't need no friends."

I shrug. "Suit yourself." I make my way up the alley to the side street. A pair of headlights throw beams onto the otherwise empty street, reflecting off the wet pavement. The cab pulls up next to me, and I hop into the back seat. "Waiting long?" I ask Cam.

"Not really. I had a couple of fares tonight so I've been busy. So what's the scoop, boss?"

I settle back as the cab takes off down the road. "Well, I don't think Moe, the bartender, is involved. And I didn't find the ring. I got bored casing the crowd, and I got a couple of strange looks from a couple of guys." I yawn. "You up for watching the treehouse again?"

"Sure. What's so special about it?"

"Moe says it's used for weddings."

"Someone we know getting married?"

"Not that I know of. I just think it's being used for more than that. I want to know who. I think there's something much bigger going on than just the attempts on my life."

"What's bigger than your life?"

"I'd rather not say until I'm sure."

"Give me a hint."

"You'll be one of the first to know. I promise. So can you keep an eye on the treehouse tomorrow?"

"No problem. What are you going to do?"

"Me?" I hadn't thought that far. "I need to check in with the editor, see if he has anything he wants me to work on. If not, I think I'll visit Congressman Dolby again."

"Are you going to need a ride?"

"I'll make do with another cab. I want you to watch that treehouse. I'll check in with you tomorrow."

29

"So have you heard about the march this weekend?" I follow Dolby's servant down the hall.

His back stiffens."Yes, sir."

"What do you think about it?"

"It's not my place to say, sir."

"Some people don't like the future."

"Me, sir?"

"No. The Klan."

"Yes, sir." He announces me to the Congressman who is again sitting behind his desk. Apart from a change of clothes, it could have been the first day I was here.

"Well? What is it now? I'm a busy man."

"I'm sure you are. Did you get a chance to see the story on the exhibit?"

His demeanor relaxes and is visibly relieved."Yes. I want to thank you for keeping me out of it. I'm sure the artists are grateful for the publicity as well. Now, what is this visit about?" He eyes me with suspicion.

"I just have some questions about the treehouse in the back of the Krazy Kat Klub."

His eyes narrow."Treehouse? How would I know? Why don't you go talk to the owner or the proprietor. I just set up the exhibit there. I don't run the place."

"Oh? Well I talked to the bartender, Moe. He said he wasn't the owner."

"Well you should ask him who the owner is. Why are you wasting my time?"

"I did."

"And?" His anger is evident as is his snarl.

"He said he couldn't tell me." I pause a beat. "I think he could, he just wouldn't."

"Well, what are you implying?"

I backed off. "Nothing. I was just wondering if you knew who it was since you probably had to deal with them to set things up."

He glares at me. "I dealt exclusively with the bartender—Moe you said was his name?"

"Oh, OK. Well if you can't tell me, you can't. Sorry for wasting your time."

"Good day."

I feel his glare drill into my back as I leave the office once again escorted by the servant. "The Congressman's not in a good mood today, is he?"

"No, sir. He never is."

"Why do you work for him then?"

"One has to pay the bills and support the family, sir."

I exit, but before I do the servant stops me. "Thank you, sir."

"For what?"

"What you said earlier, sir. About the future. I never thought of it that way."

I nod, then walk down the short path to the street. I check my watch. It's almost noon and my stomach verifies with a growl. I turn onto the sidewalk and head to a sandwich joint a few blocks away. The sun is out between large fluffy white clouds and the streets are drying. My mood, however, is stormy. Dolby was definitely lying about being the boss of the club. He was also lying about the treehouse. Somehow I had to prove he was lying otherwise it was his word against mine. I had to prove he was selling bootleg gin and had me thrown into the Anacostia. If I couldn't do that I didn't have a story.

Footsteps behind me grabbed my attention as did the pain at the back of my skull before I passed out.

30

I wake up in darkness. My head has blown off, or it feels as if it has. I lay on hard ground and on my back. There is no sky. I'm inside. I try to move, but pain stops me. I groan. My wrists and ankles are bound. A rope cuts into my skin, but I can ignore it because of the pain in my head. It takes several minutes for my mind to clear enough to recall who I was and what had happened. What had happened? Someone had clobbered me—that's what. The pain fades to a dull throb. I sit up and look around. A wave of dizziness washes over me. I want to retch, but I don't want to throw up all over myself, even in the dark. I swallow hard. I scan the area; the darkness resolves into stone pillars as my eyes adjust to the dark. I have no clue where I am. Square shapes several dozen yards away catch my eye. I look up. The roof is distant. I'm in some sort of warehouse. The nearest warehouses were near the Potomac. I bring my hands up to my eyes. I can make out the rope that binds them. I'd have to find something to cut myself free.

I struggle to stand, but the rope around my ankles throws me off balance several times. I fall. The pain of falling pulls my attention away from my head. I fight upright again until I balance enough to hop toward the crates. I lean against them to regain my breath. A crowbar lies on one of the crates, but it won't cut through the rope. How long have I been out? How long have I been here? The fact I wasn't dead tells me whoever had taken the time to bring me here and tie me up wanted something from me. I have no idea what, but I guessed Congressman Dolby was the answer to who. I have to get out before they came back. Whoever they were, I knew my health would suffer.

I grasp the crowbar in both hands and pry a plank off of a crate. Archimedes never had his ankles tied when moving the world. With a grunt the board breaks free and flies behind the crate. I peer inside. The crate holds layers of bottles. I grab one between both hands and smash it against the side of the crate. I'm rewarded with a splash of gin and shards of glass. I hold the broken neck of the bottle as I slide down the crates to a sitting position until I can work the broken edge of the bottle against the rope around my ankles. The world spins as the pain in my head returns. I stop. I breathe. I probably have a concussion. I take a slow breath and put my head between my legs to keep from passing out. I cling to consciousness like a drowning man clings to a life vest. Waves of dizziness wash over me. I fight them and win. I continue to saw with the piece of glass to free my ankles and several minutes of huffing and panting reward me. I rub life into my legs with both hands and finally stand without fear of falling over.

The slamming of a door sends my heart and breath racing. I struggle to turn the broken bottle against the rope on my wrists and drop it. I fumble to retrieve the bottleneck. A door opens, casting a shaft of light into the space. The crates are thrown into stark contrast as two figures are silhouetted in the doorway. I freeze, hoping they ignore me.

"I don't get why we can't have some light."

"We aren't supposed to be here at night."

"But I can't see."

"Deal with it. We don't want to attract any attention. The boss wants to find out what the chump knows."

About what?"

"How should I know? He just wants us to work him over, then dump him."

My heart pounds into my throat. Like a madman I saw at the ropes. Like a madman, I hope. My fingers fumble the piece of glass. It tinkles against the hard floor.

"It looks like our friend's awake." They spot me in the glow from the open door. My attempts freeze. I try to fade into the darkness, but fail.

"Look! He's messed up our shipment. The boss won't be happy."

"Yeah. You remember the time we tried to deliver the stuff early?"

"How can I forget? He chewed us out bad."

I decide my best chance of escape is to make a break for it. I rush them, holding my tied hands in front of me like a battering ram. I plow into one man and send him sprawling. The other curses. I make a break for the stairs that lead up to the door. A step catches my foot and I crash face first onto the steps. My jaw takes the brunt of the impact. I pass out.

I come to. I hurt again. I hurt more than before. I focus but see nothing. I've been blindfolded. I struggle against the fresh ropes that now hold me to a chair.

"He's awake." The voice belongs to one of the two men I'd heard before.

"Yeah. Now maybe we can get on with it."

My heart threatens to beat out of my chest. "Who are you?" I croak.

"I'm the one asking the questions." The harsh response comes from the other man.

"Where am I?" I ask, then buckle under the slap that hits me in the darkness.

"He doesn't learn fast, does he?"

"I told you we're the ones asking the questions."

"What do you want to know?" I cough through the pain. Another slap flings my head to the side.

"I told you we're the ones asking questions." His companion's chuckle is evil. I grunt more from the pain than as an acknowledgment.

"You should stop meddling in affairs that don't concern you."

"I—I don't know what you mean." I gasp as my breath returns.

"Don't play dumb. We know you've been poking your nose where it don't belong. What have you found out? You was snooping around. You're a troublemaker."

"I don't know what you're talking about." The slap resounds in the warehouse. It rings in my head.

"Tell us what you know."

"I know a lot." My response is a mumble. Another slap causes me to fight to stay conscious.

"You think you're a smart alec. We'll see how smart you are after we rough you up some more." I collapse on the chair as the blows hit my stomach. The beating continues for several long seconds. "Now then. Tell us what you know?"

I can't focus. "About what?", I groan.

"What do you know about the booze?"

"What booze? I—" I cough and taste blood. "I don't know anything about booze."

Another slap brings my attention into focus. "The gin and whiskey. You know what I mean. Don't play dumb." Whiskey? My mind whirls.

"I know nothing about whiskey."

"Why do you hang around the Krazy Kat Klub then?"

I took a deep breath. "I was writing an article about the art exhibit. I —I don't—they don't even sell whiskey."

I hear a grunt. "Why were you askin' about the boss?"

"I don't even know who the boss is. I think it's Congressman Dolby. Is it?" A punch to my gut forces the air out of my lungs.

"We know you've been nosing around. You've got no sense for a fluff reporter. You should stick to covering weddings and museums. Speakeasys can be dangerous places. So how much do you know? Spill it, Blackie."

I spit in the voice's direction. I pass out from the blow to the side of my head.

31

I roll onto my back and cough. My eyes feel as if they are glued together as I force them open. I have no clue how long I've been out. A gray shaft of light illuminates motes of dust that hang in the air and twinkle like tiny fireflies. I push myself upright and am surprised to find I am no longer bound. Frantically, I scan the dim light of the warehouse but see no signs of my captors. Still, my heart and breathing race. I stand waiting, maybe for the two men to spring out at me, or for the pain to subside, neither of which happens. After what seems like an hour, I feel my emotions relax enough so that I'm no longer gasping in a panic. For whatever reason, the two had left me–maybe they thought I was dead, or maybe they felt they had taught me a lesson. Either way, I am relieved and grateful the beating has stopped. I glance around the warehouse, hoping to find something that would tell me who the two men were. But the only incriminating evidence is the crates of bottles. That's enough. It's something I can report to the police and everything would be wrapped up. They can tie the warehouse and the illegal liquor to Dolby.

I shuffle to the door as wave after wave of pain and dizziness wash over me. I stand bracing myself against the door frame until my head clears. Someone wants me out of the way. Someone is afraid I'd found something I shouldn't have. Was it Dolby? I'm pretty certain it is. Was it the gin and whiskey? Probably. From the questioning the two had given me, I was pretty certain that was the key. They didn't know I knew about the outfit I'd found, or they would have brought it up. Was Dolby a Klansman? Maybe. My gut tells me he is, but I have no proof. Everything I have is circumstantial.

I'll report the attack and warehouse. That's proof, along with my injuries, but I'm certain Dolby is too smart to leave a trail back to him. Taking a deep breath, I hobble out and look for a ride home.

32

Several hours later, after a quick trip to the E.R. to make sure I was OK, washed, and with a change of clothes, I knock on Tayla's door. It swings open. Tayla's smile quickly changes to an expression of shock when she sees my face. "Randy, what happened?"

My grin is lopsided. "I ran into a couple of guys who didn't like my sense of humor."

"Are you OK? Come on in! You look awful."

"Thanks. I feel worse than I look."

"Maybe you should go to the hospital."

"Already been there. I'm OK." We sit on the chaise.

Tayla places a hand on my arm. "Does it hurt much?"

I retell my last couple of days. She sits listening, then when I am done, throws her arms around me and gives me a long kiss. I feel better. "Do you really think Goody—Goodwin is behind it all? He wants to see me again."

"Certain. He's the kingpin. But, I wish I could find out who the guy with the ring and two thugs are. It would make tying them together easier." I frown. "Did he say why?"

She shakes her head. The pony tail she wears flounces back and forth. "No. He probably still thinks I'm his girlfriend." Her voice drips in disgust. "I never want to see him again." She takes my hands in hers and shifts closer. "I'm not his girlfriend." Her eyes lock onto mine.

I hate myself but I say, "You should see him again." Tayla lets go and flinches back.

"Why? I don't want anything to do with him! Why would you want me to go back to that vile man?"

"I said go see him. I don't want you to be his girlfriend."

"Why?" She crosses her arms over her chest. "The thought of him makes my skin crawl."

"I know. I hate the idea too, but if he wants to see you, you should go. I want you to scope out if he knows about the warehouse."

Tayla's eyes grow wide. "How am I supposed to do that?"

I sit on the chaise in silence. I hadn't thought things through and feel like a dummy. I get an idea. "Just get him talking—about whiskey. Ask him if you can have a shot."

"I hate whiskey."

"You don't have to drink it. Just ask for a shot. Then if he gives it to you, get him talking about where he gets it. If he mentions the warehouse that will tie him and the two the thugs who clobbered me."

"What if he doesn't have whiskey?"

I shrug. "I'll have to come up with something else." I look at her sitting next to me. I'm running out of options. "I hate asking you to do this. I know the type of person he is and what he's capable of."

"Isn't there some other way?" Her eyes plead, and I hesitate.

"You don't have to do this if you don't want to but it would help me get the goods on the guy." She looks at me and nods without saying anything. "Good girl." I lean over and kiss her forehead. "Just be safe. If you think you're in any danger, I want you to make a beeline out of there. Got it?"

"Got it. Believe me, I don't want to stay there any longer than I have to."

"I owe you, babe."

"You owe me big." She sighs. "I have to move out. I can't stay here anymore." She looks around the lavishly furnished but small apartment. "I've grown used to this place. But every night I stay here reminds me of him." A shiver passes through her.

I'm not sure how to say it so I come out and spill it. "You can stay with me."

Her head tilts, and she looks at me askance. "What would people think? Or were you thinking of making me an honest woman?"

I gulp as sweat breaks out on my upper lip. I recover. "Babe, it's 1925. Guys are living with guys in New York without raising much of an eyebrow."

"They are?" Tayla's voice holds shock and wonder. Half a beat passes. "Have you?"

"What? Been roomies with a guy? No! Of course not. I'm not into that sort of thing, but live and let live I say."

She seems relieved. "You're not doing this just to pay me back, are you?"

"Pay you back? Oh, for scoping out Dolby? Don't be silly. I care about you." She smiles and moves closer.

33

The next day, I'm back in the yellow. "I've got something for you."
Cam announces from the front seat of his cab,

"You saw someone go up into the treehouse?" I shift my gaze from
the traffic to the rear-view mirror.

"Yeah. I was just hanging around the club. It was jumpin' last night.
I had a couple of drinks and was sitting out on the terrace. I heard
voices. I ducked behind the wall. A guy came out and went up into the
tree house."

"And?"

"He came down."

"That's it?"

"Yeah."

"Did you see who it was?"

Cam shrugs in front of me."Have no idea. He was big and burley. It
was too dark to see his face. I couldn't tell who it was."

"Did you follow him?"

"I didn't have to. He went back into the office through the back. It
sounded like there was someone already there."

"Dolby?"

"Couldn't see."

"Too bad. Was he carrying anything when he came down from the
tree house?"

"Carrying something? No, not that I could see. He just came down
and went into the office."

"What then?"

"Nothing. I hung around until last call. The place closed up, but there was still a light in the back office. I got tired and went home."

"Good job. Big and burley, you said? I hoped you could ID the Congressman, but the description fits him. It's still circumstantial, though. You didn't catch a glimpse of the ring, did you?"

"No, boss. No ring. What next?"

"Swing by the Dolby mansion. Tayla should be coming out soon. I want to make sure she's OK. I had her check out something for me."

"Sure thing."

The cab takes a left and heads toward O Street. I sit in the back mulling over the new info. Dolby had gone into the tree house. The Klan march on D.C. was tomorrow. He must've gotten the outfit in order to get ready. Having the outfit didn't prove he was a Klansman. Somehow, I had to prove he was one. I still had nothing the cops could use; certainly nothing they could use against a congressman. The cab arrives at the mansion. I had arranged with Tayla that I'd pick her up, but there is no sign of her. Cam and I sit and wait. Time passes and I glance at my watch, as I had done every few minutes for an hour. The sun is sinking behind a large black cloud in the west.

"Boss, I don't think she's coming."

"You're right, Cam. Something must've happened." I swing the door open and step onto the curb. "I'm going to go see if she's still in there. Hang around for a while. If I'm not out in half an hour call the cops."

34

I walk up to the porch and knock. A moment later, the servant opens the door. "Has Tayla Bourke been here?", I ask.

"Yes, sir. The young lady was here and left a while ago."

"Did she seem OK?"

"Ok, sir? I don't understand."

"Upset. Did she seem upset?"

"Not that I could tell, sir."

"Is the Congressman in?"

"Yes, sir. But he is not accepting any more visitors today."

I stand on the porch, unsure what to do. I have an idea. "Could you tell the Congressman that I have some important information for him? Tell him—tell him it concerns a warehouse." The servant says nothing but turns and disappears into the house. I stand, wait and think about whether I am making a mistake.

The man returns quickly. "Congressman Dolby will see you." I'm led again to the office.

"I'm told you have some information for me about a warehouse? Why would I care about a warehouse?" There is no greeting and his voice and demeanor are cold.

"I just wanted to follow up on a rumor I heard."

"A rumor?"

"That you own a warehouse on the Potomac."

"Really? I don't."

"And that it was being used to store illegal whiskey."

"I told you I don't own any warehouses. And as a Congressman I know selling and serving alcoholic beverages is illegal."

"Good. Good. I'm glad to hear it."

"Now if you will excuse me, I have a party to go to and I have to get ready."

"Sure. Sure. I'm sorry to have bothered you." I turn to leave, then stop. "Oh, one more thing. You haven't seen Tayla Bourke, the artist lately, have you?"

He glares at me. "No. Should I have?"

"No. I was just wondering. I wanted to do a follow-up story on her and her art." I lied poorly.

"I told you, no. Now please leave before I have you thrown out."

I follow the manservant out to the main entrance.

Once out of earshot of the office, he says, "I couldn't help but overhear your conversation, sir. I don't eavesdropping but your voices were loud." I grunt acknowledgment. "The Congressman did see Miss Bourke as I stated before."

"Do you know what they talked about?"

"No sir. As I said, I don't eavesdrop."

"Of course not. Thank you."

"My pleasure, sir."

35

I walk out to the yellow and jump into the back. "Tayla must've gone home. Let's head there."

"I don't think so." The muzzle of a vicious-looking Browning points at my face from the front seat. My heart skips a beat.

"Who are you? What do you want?" Before I can get an answer, the passenger side of the cab opens and a large man slips into the seat beside me. Another Browning now faces my stomach.

"Let's go." The newcomer nods at the driver. "I have him."

"What do you want? Who are you?"

"Shut up. You'll find out soon enough." I don't recognize either of the men.

"What—what did you do with Cam?"

"The driver? He's taking a nap in the trunk."

"You killed him?"

"Nah. He'll just have a nasty headache when he wakes up."

"Where are we going?" I talk to calm my terror.

The muzzle digs into my ribs. "Shut up. You keep poking your nose where it don't belong." I shut up. I glance at the lethal piece of metal that held my life in the balance. A street lamp reflects a yellow glow that catches my eye. The man next to me wears a ring. I stare at it to make sure I'm not imagining it. The rod in my gut keeps me from asking. The hand the ring is attached to belongs to a burly man with a large mustache. His clothes are nothing to write home about. They are matted and dirty, worker's clothes.

The cab drives out of D.C. to a small house in Arlington. The Browning waves to indicate I'm to exit and I'm not about to argue. The two men follow close behind as I am led inside and pushed into a wooden chair in the first room. It's bare apart from an old oil lamp and the chair. I'm quickly bound to the chair.

"So why were you nosing around the Krazy Kat Klub? The truth. We know about the news story you wrote. That won't fly here."

My co-passenger points the Browning at me. "That's the only reason. What other reason could there be?"

"Yeah, right, and I'm the Pope." The second thug's chuckle is evil.

"We're asking you nicely. Why were you nosing around the club? Why are you hassling the Congressman?"

"Congressman? What Congressman?" A slap across my face twists my head. My still-healing bruises scream.

"We don't like doing things this way. If you tell the truth, you'll suffer much less. Why are you hassling the Congressman?"

"Who are you guys?" I struggle through the pain. "Why did you dump me in the river?"

"What the hell are you talking about? What do you know about the Congressman. We're not going to ask you again."

"I—I think he's scamming artists." My admission comes out as a groan. My mind is sluggish from the pain. Maybe if I offer them that they will stop hitting me.

"Scamming artists?"

"Ye—yes. He charges to show their art, but he's making more off of them than they get back. He charges them $50 a month." Another slap across my jaw.

"What else?"

I struggle to answer. My mouth feels numb and my vision blurs. "I —I don't know anything else. That's it." My voice comes out in a weak growl.

The two men watch me for a moment, then move off to the side of the room and whisper to one another. A few moments later, they face me again. "We're only going to say this once. Stop messing with things you know nothing about. Stay with reporting fluff. Otherwise, you might get hurt." The driver pulls a knife out of a cabinet drawer and tosses it on my lap. "Have a nice day." The two men leave the house. A moment later, the sound of a car racing away tells me I'm on my own.

36

I free myself after several minutes and this time I don't have to crash to the floor. I stagger out into the night and breathe a sigh of relief when I see the outline of the yellow. My mind freezes when I remember Cam is locked in the trunk. I rush to the cab and pull the keys from the ignition. I pop open the trunk and see the still body of Cam. A quick check of his pulse and breathing tells me he's still alive. I struggle through my pain to pull him out of the trunk and flop him down on the rear seat. I limp back into the house and find a metal cup, which I fill with water. I return to Cam and bring him around. He moans as I put the cup to his lips.

"Which train hit me?"

"You'll be OK. Just take it easy."

Cam sits up suddenly. "Where is he? Where's the bum who clobbered me with a blackjack?"

"They're gone. Relax. You've been in the trunk for a while. What happened?"

"I'll be OK." He rubs the back of his head. "Ouch! Apart from a nasty bump. I was sitting there waiting for you to come out when this guy slips into the back seat. I thought he was just a passenger looking for a lift. I told him I was off duty. Next thing I know I get smacked in the head, and then I wake up here. How long was I out?"

"A few hours."

He looks up at me in the moonlight. "What happened to you?"

"Don't ask. We're in Arlington. Can you drive, or do you want me to?"

Cam stands up "I'm OK. I can drive. Do you know who got us?"

"A couple of guys. I'm not sure. I didn't recognize them. They wanted to know what I knew. I didn't give them much."

"Sounds like a rough bunch. If it's worth anything, I didn't recognize the guy in the cab when I got slugged. Who do you think they are?"

"I don't know, but I'm betting Dolby's bunch. One thing I do know is one of them had the ring."

37

"Listen. I want to help. I really do. But I can't." The sergeant shrugs. "I sent a patrol car to check out the warehouse. When we got there, it was empty. If there were any cases of whiskey or anything else, they were gone. Same with the house in Arlington. Nothing. That's been abandoned for about a year."

"Gone? Are you sure?" My hopes of getting some concrete evidence are dashed like a whiskey bottle on the road.

"Why would I lie? Right now, you have a lot of bruises. I can't argue you weren't beat up. But, unless you know who they were we can't do a thing."

"I know. I know." I'm frustrated. I blurt before I can stop, "if I were anyone else...", then catch myself.

"If that's all, the Klan's coming into town and we're going to be busy here."

"Do you expect trouble?"

"I hope not, but we have to be ready."

"Oh, one other thing. Have you heard of a special ring some of the Feds wear?" He shakes his head. I mumble as I walk out of the station, "Thanks anyway."

38

I walk out into the early morning sun. Traffic is heavier than usual; my guess is a lot of people are coming into town for the march. I turn the corner and walk home. My mind swims in my thoughts. My body hurts. I've been tossed in the river and beaten up twice by thugs. I ask myself why I'm doing this. What had started out as a piece on an exhibit has nearly cost me my life. Maybe the thugs are right. Maybe I should stop nosing around and stick to what I do best. After all, I'm not an investigative reporter. My stories are always buried in the second or third section of the paper. I should quit, but I have a lot of clues that I can't put together. My face is swollen and beaten. Strangers stare at me, then quickly look away as they pass me on the street. Two little old ladies whisper to each other, then scurry away like frightened rabbits when I stare at them. Now I know what it feels like to be an outsider, an outcast, more than usual. My mood is as dark as the sky and my skin.

I arrive home and find a note on my door. Tayla wants to see me. I'd forgotten she had gone to see Dolby. I'm glad she's OK. I'd also forgotten I'd said she could move in with me. Pain does that. I go out again and hail a cab. I figure Cam deserves a rest after what he'd gone through. I deserve a break as well and I plan to take it. Knowing I'd be taking it with Tayla makes the prospect more enticing. I wasn't getting paid to track down clues while getting beaten up. And what I was getting paid for writing wasn't enough. Why did I care if some Congressman was running a speakeasy and bootleg? Or that same Congressman was a Klansman and had hired a bunch of thugs to get rid of me. Well, I did care, but not enough to keep trying. Life was too short, and I didn't want to make it any shorter.

"This the place?" The cabbie turns to me in front of Tayla's.

"Yeah. Thanks."

He quotes the fare then adds, "You worried about the march?"

"No."

"I am, and you should be. The country is going to hell in a handbasket if you ask me." I agree.

39

Tayla throws her arms around me, and we lock in a long kiss. I forget about my pain. She pulls back when I flinch as she squeezes me. "What's wrong?", she asks as she examines my face. "Oh, you poor dear! What happened? You have new bruises."

"New clobbering. Never mind that. How'd the visit to Dolby go?"

She leads me to the chaise where we both sit. "I did as you said. I went in and he was all lovey-dovey like he didn't remember hitting me."

"Or he didn't care."

She grimaces. "Anyway, he wanted to know if I wanted to go to Atlantic City for the weekend with him." I feel my anger rise. She continues, "I told him no. I told him I had to visit my grandmother."

"Did he buy that?"

Tayla nods. "He was upset I couldn't go, but he didn't push me. Then I pretended to be dizzy and said I was going to faint. I asked for a drink. He wanted to get me water, but I asked for something stronger." She pauses for effect. "Well, he brought me a shot of whiskey. He told me that's the only thing he had in the house."

"So he at least has illegal liquor at home, and whiskey at that. Gin for the club, whiskey at home. He can sell gin at a higher profit."

"I acted all surprised. I asked him how he could get alcohol when it was illegal."

"And?"

"Well, he hemmed and hawed and said being a Congressman had special perks."

"I bet. Anything else?"

"No. We just talked a bit more about the trip to Atlantic City and I said I was really sorry that I couldn't go. Then I left. I was there for just a few minutes. When I got out onto the street you weren't there and I thought standing around a street corner for half an hour would attract too much attention."

"Good girl. But, I was worried when we didn't find you there. I'm glad you're OK. So are you ready to move in?" She nods and gives me another painful hug. "Watch it! I'm still recovering"

She eases up but doesn't let go. "Are you sure you want me?"

"Baby, I'm more sure than I have been of anything else. Need help packing?"

"No. I can do it. Can I move in tomorrow?"

"Today. Tomorrow. It's all good as long as you do."

"I should get my art from the club."

"I'll do that. I'll pick it up tomorrow night. Ok?"

"I should also probably let Congressman Dolby know I'm moving out." She purses her lips. "He probably won't be happy."\

She was right. Knowing him, he'd be furious. "You can leave a note."

"Will that work?"

"Why not?" She gives me a light peck on my cheek, being careful to avoid the bruise. She was happy. I like it when she is happy. Shouts from outside catch our attention. We look at each other, puzzled. I walk to the front window and peer out. Tayla stands next to me. A sea of white cones moves down the street chanting and shouting.

"What is it? What's going on?" Tayla draws closer to me.

"It's the Klan. They're marching on D.C. today." My skin crawls at the thought of the racist gathering.

"The Klan? You mean the KKK? How awful! Why do they let them march like that in those awful robes and hoods?"

I shrug. "It's their right, I guess. They're still citizens. As long as they don't cause trouble, they can march all they want. But something tells me it won't stay peaceful."

"I don't like it. I'm afraid."

I look at at the hooded anonymous men moving past us, shouting and chanting at anyone within sight or earshot. I pull her closer. "That's what they want. They want us to fear them and what they represent. But they are the ultimate cowards. They hide their faces behind symbols because they are small people." She looked up at me questioning. I continue, "Good people have to stand together as well.

If we stand tight enough, there will be no room for hate and lies." I kiss her. There is no Klan, no corrupt Congressman, no space, no pain.

40

Later that evening, I go out to grab a bite to eat and clear my head. The sky's a dark shade of slate, full of roiling clouds that drop buckets of chilly water. As I walk down the street toward the deli a block away, my mind focuses on Tayla and what I had gotten myself into. Bits of trash from the Klan march stick to the pavement like a lover, not wanting to lose its mate. Rain streams from my hair and down my face in rivulets, mixing with the hard drops that splash onto me as I turn the corner and run headlong into a guy in his mid-thirties.

"Watch where yer goin'!", the man roars. His speech slurs and I smell the booze on his breath as he shoves me back.

"Well looky here, Jake," his younger companion begins. "We got us here a Blackie." The man who pushed me peers at me through his haze of booze. He runs an arm under his nose to wipe the rain away. He fails. He blinks, staring at me, then his mind seems to engage a low gear.

"Yer right, Paul. This boy done run into me and not a damn word of apology. These big city –", he used the "N" word. My thoughts of Tayla, Dolby, and woes are wiped clean from my consciousness as rage and anger flare with the brightness of the noonday sun. Jake–or was it Paul–continues. "… don't know their place. We should teach this one some manners." The younger man glances around as he takes an inebriated step toward me. "Too bad we don't got no rope. Guess we'll just have to give this one a whoopin'."

My hands have instinctively balled into fists, and my sight is going red despite the black sky and rain. The older of the two takes a step toward me. "You, boy, are going to learn your place. We'll teach you to disrespect your betters." The younger one takes a position next to his companion.

"Yeah–, you'll know your place, right under the heel of my boot." He lifts his foot and points at the rain-drenched wingtip shoe. He stumbles as he does, grabbing at his friend to catch his balance. The two of them advance toward me along the deserted street, cursing, taunting, and degrading me. "Apologize, boy, and you might get out of this alive," the younger spits at me as he pulls a small evil-looking knife out of his jeans pocket. My rage is already at an all-time high. The n-word had triggered something deep within me. I brace myself to attack, knowing there is no way I'd let these two get me without a fight.

The man I'd run into moves unsteadily toward me. His fist flies toward my face. Without thinking, I grab his wrist in both my hands and yank as hard as I can. The man hurtles by me, an astonished look on his face. I don't have a chance to see where he lands because the man with the knife curses and lunges. The knife swooshes past my ear as I duck; the swing pulls the man off-balance to my right. Before he can recover, I come up and slam my shoulder against his. The knife topples into the middle of the street and clatters against the pavement. My opponent staggers back from the blow, but doesn't fall. Growling, he regains his footing and throws himself at me. We tumble to the sidewalk. I push him off me and roll from under him. As I do, I swing my fist down onto his rib cage but miss, hitting his stomach instead. The man yelps, grasping for my hair. He grabs hold of a few strands as I'm still moving away from him. Pain shoots through me as the clump is yanked out of my scalp. Cursing, I don't know what, I kick and scream as I lay on the ground. I hit his thigh. But that does little if any harm. The man grabs hold of my neck in both hands and squeezes.

I struggle to breathe, grasping at his wrists as I try to roll further away, but his stronger build keeps his grip and pressure on my neck. Desperate for air, I thrash with no plan or strategy. I fight to survive. My opponent's face is even with mine. Alcohol, rage, and hate-filled eyes drill into mine. His eyes are all my dimming vision sees. I slam my head into his. My head rings as I feel his grip on me loosen. Pulling his hands away with the last bits of energy left to me. I gasp for air, my vision clears and I see my assailant, his eyes unfocused on the ground next to me. I take advantage and shove him away and scramble to my feet. I kick him in the side. He curls up into a ball and howls in pain. I glance around, looking for help, but the street is still empty apart from the other man, who is groggily getting up to his feet.

Gasping heavily, I check my options and then run as fast as I can back toward my apartment. I'd survived.

41

"How's it going, boss?" I slide into the back seat of Cam's cab.

"Healing. Slowly. How about you? You still want to drive me around after what we went through?"

The toothpick twitches. "What? Being conked on the noggin and thrown in the trunk?" He makes a noise that sounds like "pssh". "That's nothin' when you're a cabbie. I've heard worse. One day I'll have to tell you about the cabbie whose wife ground him up and put his remains into the tank." I flinch. I'm not sure if he's kidding. "Besides, I haven't had, what one might call, an adventurous life." I see Cam's grin in the mirror. The toothpick shifts sides as he asks, "Where to?"

"The Krazy Kat Klub. I need to pick up Tayla's art."

"You're really sweet on the dame, aren't you?"

"Yeah, I am."

"Sure she's not trouble?"

"Life is trouble."

"That's deep, boss. Did you see the march yesterday?"

"Yeah." I explain what happened. Cam shakes his head, but says nothing. I ask, "Did you? What did you think?"

"Yeah. They shut down some of the streets. It cost me a lot of fares, what with them all walkin'." The toothpick sits on his lower lip, motionless. "It's a crazy world we live in. Some person hates some other person. They get together and a whole bunch of people hate another whole bunch of people. Next thing you know we have a war."

"That's deep, Cam."

He grins into the rear-view. "I have my moments. You want me to do some more snooping?"

I think for a moment. "Nah. You've done enough. I'm giving up."

"Giving up?" He stares at me then swerves to avoid a car as a result. He curses. "What do you mean, giving up? Like quitting?"

"Just that. I'm tired of getting dunked and clobbered. Those guys weren't playing around, you know." I shiver at the memory of the Browning.

"What about truth, justice, and the law? Don't those hoods deserve to be locked up?"

"Yeah, they do. But it's not my job to do it." Cam shakes his head in front of me. He says nothing. I continue, "I'd love to get whoever it is behind bars. But, I'm just one guy. What can I do?" Silence. "Listen, I have a good thing going with Tayla. I have a decent job. It doesn't pay much, but I get by. I don't want to mess it up."

"I get it, boss. I just didn't think you were the kind of guy to run out."

"I'm not running out. I'm quitting."

"We're here. Do you want me to hang around?"

"Please."

42

I leave the yellow and walk down the alley to the club. I'm on my own and it feels like I've just lost a friend. I shrug in the muggy night air. My clothes cling to me like Tayla had, but not as comforting. I walk down the alley to where Jericho Waldroup again stands guard over the entrance.

"You know the drill." He's more surly than usual, if that's possible. His pat down is more thorough and personal than before.

I snarl, "Hey, watch it, bub!"

"Need to make sure you're not here to cause trouble. We've had a couple of white hood types try to sneak rods into the place. You know the rule, no Feds, no cops, no guns."

"Yeah."

"You're clean. You can go in." I move toward the door and hear the band. Waldroup calls after me, "You haven't seen Tayla, have you?"

I stop in my tracks. "Tayla?"

"Yeah. I saw you getting chummy with her the first night you were here. She's a square kid. I haven't seen her around. Just want to make sure she's OK."

"Oh. She hasn't been here? Sorry. I wouldn't know. I got thrown into the river and lost touch with her." I didn't feel like explaining things to a doorman.

"Sorry to hear. Have a nice night."

I'm perplexed. The bouncer seemed genuine, even if rough. I enter the smoke filled club.

43

The place is packed and noisier than I'd ever seen it. A fog of acrid smoke hangs in the air. My eyes sting as I push my way through the crowd, around the edge of the dance floor. Loud laughter and chatter give the club a constant din of noise. The booze is flowing tonight. I reach Moe, who stands placidly behind the bar. "Back again? The usual?"

"Whiskey if you have it." I decide to tempt fate.

"Sorry, just water."

"That'll do. You're busy today. What's the occasion?"

He shrugs as he pours the liquid. "People in to see the march. People in the march, I guess."

"You let them in?"

"It's not like we ask to see their hoods you know."

"So you don't approve of the Klan?"

He glares at me. "Do you?"

"No. I'm like you. I don't go in much for slavery and whites for whites. The world is changing."

He relaxes. "I hope so. So you here doing another story?"

"No. I'm here to pick up Tayla Bourke's art for her."

Moe peers at me for several moments. "Is she OK? Why are you picking up Tayla's stuff?"

"She asked me to."

"She's OK? What's she up to? Why doesn't she pick it up herself?"

I pause, unsure how to respond, then say, "She's still not feeling well. I called her number, and she asked me to get her stuff."

Moe looks at me as if to ask, "Why you?" He puts the glass down in front of me with more force than is required. "You can't have it. She has to pick it up in person."

"Why?"

"Boss's orders. No sales or removal of the art without his say so."

"Can I talk to the boss then?"

"No."

"Why not?"

"You're not the artist."

"Is he in?" I indicate the back office with a tilt of my head. Moe glances over to the door.

"No." I can tell he's lying. I nod and walk away into the crowd. Maybe I can take Tayla's art off the walls and walk out. The place is packed and no one would notice in the noise and bodies. I wouldn't get past the man at the door, however, so I'd have to get permission. I promised Tayla I'd get her stuff today. Somehow. I push my way through the revellers and walk through an area where the heavy smoke mixes with perfume. My eyes burn and water. An aging matron sits laughing with a man half her age. I push on.

Sudden yelling in the far corner of the room catches my attention. A black couple is being harassed and insulted. Pushing and shoving ensues. Fists fly. A few people around the confrontation get involved and a moment later Moe and a couple of large men rush in to separate the combatants. A few customers stand and watch, but most ignore the ruckus. The band keeps playing. The back office door is unguarded, and I see my chance. I move to the door, taking the confusion as cover and pull the door open.

The back room is larger than I had thought. Crates stand floor to ceiling and in the center is a wooden desk, chair, and a filing cabinet. But no one is in the room. I'd hoped to catch Dolby at the club, but have failed. Cursing, I close the door before Moe gets back on-station. I blend back into the crowd just in time to see him and the bouncers manhandle the person who had attacked the black couple out of the club.

A few moments later Moe is back behind the bar. I look for my glass and discover I've left it on the bar. I move to get it. Moe glances at me. "Need a refill?

I point to the glass that sits on one corner of the wooden surface. "Left it here." I tilt my head in the direction of the fight. "What was that about?"

"Some chump was harassing a black couple. Like I said, we serve everyone here. We don't judge as long as you can pay and don't cause trouble. We don't need trouble. The guy and his pals broke the second rule. I can do without partying KKKers." I grunt agreement and take a sip of the gin.

"So no way to get Tayla's artwork without her doing it?"

"You don't want to be one of the people that break the second rule, do ya?" He glares at me.

"No. I guess not."

"Good."

"Why doesn't Tayla come in and get her stuff herself? I'd like to see her."

I shrug. "Like I said, she's sick. And she doesn't like the owner."

"If you talk to her, tell her to come in herself."

I nod and take my drink to lean against the wall.

44

The crowd goes back to their partying after the commotion. All the tables are full tonight and it's just as well since I can stand and observe from a distance. The band picks up the tempo to get everyone back in the mood. I'm not. I just want to get out and back to Tayla. I watch as an elderly gentleman dressed in a tux dances with his equally elderly wife—or maybe just a girlfriend. It's hard to tell nowadays. It's the twentieth century, and the world is changing.

A babe sits alone at a table. There is a crowd of would-be suitors preening around her. I was that young once. She flirts and laughs with all of them. Each of the men thinks her attention is only on him. That's what I had thought. She'll pick one and crush the hopes of everyone else around her. That's how it worked with me. I'm not in a good mood and am feeling sorry for myself. I shake off the funk and take a swig of the gin; it makes me feel better. The large form of Jericho Waldroup, the bouncer, moving through the crowd toward the bar catches my attention. He goes behind the bar and speaks to Moe. The club is too loud to make out what they say. Moe heads into the back room and returns a minute later. The two men exchange a couple more words as Moe hands Jericho an envelope. Jericho opens it to reveal a wad of dough. He stands, counting it. He nods, then stuffs the envelope full of bills into his inside jacket pocket. The large man then moves back through the crowd and back outside. The sour expression on Moe's face tells me he isn't happy. I move from my spot against the wall, back to the bar. I set the glass down and point at it. Moe refills it. "So what was that all about?"

"What?"

"You and Jericho. What was that about?"

Moe eyes me with suspicion. "Nothing."

"You don't seem happy. What was the money for?"

Moe's eyes narrow. "Just his weekly pay. It's payday." I nod.

A bouncer must make more in a week than I do in a year, I think. "It looked like a lot of green."

"What's it to you? You a Fed?"

"No. Just wish I could make that much." Moe glares at me. I decide I shouldn't press my luck. I take my glass and move back to my spot against the wall. The babe has chosen one of the guys and the two are dancing. He doesn't look like much. They never do. In fact, he was the plainest of the bunch that had surrounded her. She had found her sucker and would play him for all he was worth. She'd dump him and find another chump. That's how it had worked with me. I down the glass of "water" in one gulp. It stings.

I have to confront Dolby in the club. That's the only way to get enough witnesses to prove the Congressman's connection to the bootleg operation, but it wouldn't be tonight. I walk out into the night. Jericho, the bouncer, nods as I walk past.

45

My morning cup of coffee is interrupted by a knock on the door. I open it to find Tayla standing there, burdened down by boxes in both arms and a small suitcase that sits on its side on the ground. She blows an errant strand of hair out of her eyes. I grab the largest box from her. "Thanks. My arm was falling asleep," she exhales.

"Come on in." I grab the suitcase with my free hand. "Is this all your stuff?"

"Yeah. It's not much, but it's mine." She walks in behind me. I place her things in a pile by the door. She looks around at my apartment. "It's nice. Small. But nice."

"Thanks. It's not a palace but I manage to pay the bills. Want a cup of coffee?"

"Sure. So did you get my stuff from the club?"

I pour two cups of black liquid from the pot on the stove. "No. I tried. Moe says you have to get your pictures in person. You have to get Dolby's permission first." I hand her the coffee. "Make yourself at home. This is your home now, after all."

"Thanks. What am I going to do? I spent a lot of time on those paintings. I don't want that scumbag to have them."

"I'll figure something out. We'll get them back." I take a sip. "Moe wants to see you again. Is there something going on I should know about?"

She looks up from her cup. There is surprise in her eyes. "He does?" She shakes her head. "No. Nothing. He made a play for me the first day I was there, but I brushed him off. I wonder what the story is." She reaches into the purse and pulls out a cig." She notices my frown and pushes it back into the pack. "You don't smoke, do you?"

"No. Never have. Tried it once and didn't like it. It made me sick. It's bad enough when I get home and smell like smoke."

"I guess I can try to quit if it bothers you. Have you always lived here?"

"No. I grew up in Philly. I moved here about five years ago when I got the job with the Herald."

She sits frowning. "We really don't know that much about each other."

"Having second thoughts?"

She shakes her head, then grins. "No. Not for an instant." She leans over the table and takes my hand.

"Let's get you unpacked and moved in," I say. I wrap my arms around her.

46

The next morning I once again stand in Congressman Dolby's office on O Street. "Well? What now? You're like an annoying gnat I can't get rid of." He glares at me from across his desk.

"I'm here on behalf of Tayla Bourke." His eyebrows go up. "She'd like to get her art but doesn't want to go back to the club. I tried to pick it up but Moe said the owner had to approve."

"I told you. I'm not the owner. Why are you wasting my time?"

"Let's stop playing games. You're not only in charge of the art show, but I know you're the owner of the club." I was playing a bluff, hoping he'd admit to what I guessed.

He stands up behind the desk and takes a step toward me. "And how do you know that?"

"All the artists deal directly with you to exhibit at the club."

Dolby spreads his hands wide as if apologizing. "I just set the shows up. I'm not the owner."

"Then who is? If you deal with the art, then you have to deal with the owner."

"I'm sorry but I can't help you." Dolby moves to a side table. "He prefers to stay anonymous. That's all I can say. Would you like a drink?" He lifts a carafe of wine. He'd called my bluff.

My body sags. "I'm not much of a wine man. I prefer whiskey."

"Now you know I wouldn't have whiskey. It's illegal you know."

"Yes, I was just saying I prefer it."

"Well, if you won't have a small glass, I will." He pours the wine into a crystal goblet. "Now, Mr. Cook, there's no reason for us to keep butting heads over this, is there? I'm not the owner of the Kit Kat Klub, believe me. If I could help you, I would." He moves back to his desk and sits down with the glass of wine.

"So Tayla can't get her art back even if you give permission?" The hands go wide again. "Well, we'll sue to get it back." I was being frustrated at every turn. "I'll write a story uncovering everything you're doing."

Dolby's left eyebrow shoots up again. "And what is it I'm doing? Without proof you'd just be writing rumors." He tsk tsks at me. "That wouldn't be good reporting. What would the Herald do then?" He was right. If I fulfilled my threat, I'd probably be fired. My hands clenched into fists. He takes another sip as he watches me. "Sure you don't want a glass? It's a nice vintage." I stand fuming, unable to say anything. "Well, if there is nothing else, I have work to do. Say hello to Tayla." His grin is more leer than a grin.

47

I stomp out of the house and then slide into the back of Cam's cab, slamming the door shut. "I guess no luck, huh?" he asks.

"That man is scum. He was toying with me. I even accused him of being the owner of the club."

"And?"

"He denied it. I guess I should've expected that. I even threatened to write a story, but he knows I don't have anything with which to back it up. I need to get something on him, something that will hold up."

"I thought you said you had given up."

"I did. I have. I guess I'm just upset that I couldn't get the art back."

"Uh, huh. You could always sue."

"You have to have someone to sue. That's the owner of the club."

"Didn't you say Dolby set the show up? You could sue him."

"I don't know. I'm not a lawyer. I should check on that. Thanks." The toothpick nods.

"Where to?"

"Home. I need to figure out what to do next and maybe talk to a lawyer."

The cab pulls away from the curb. A minute later he says, "We've got a tail."

I swing around in the back seat and look. A black Ford is closer to us than the light traffic called for. I can't make out the driver. "I don't feel like getting beat up again. Can you lose him?"

"Sure thing. I don't feel like taking another nap in the trunk." Cam speeds up. The car behind us does as well. The yellow turns onto a side street and the tail follows. Cam takes various turns, but the car matches every move he makes. "Persistent, isn't he?"

"I thought you said you could lose him."

"Wait. I'm just getting started. Hold on tight."

The six-cylinder engine revs and the cab springs forward, pushing me back into the seat. The car weaves between the few others on the road. I look behind and see the Ford has given chase. The cab races through an intersection. The light is red. Cars screech to a halt as we rush through. My heart pounds as we pass by the White House. The Ford keeps pace. I peer over Cam's shoulder. The gauge read thirty-five. He pulls the wheel to the right and the cab screeches into a narrow road. I catch sight of a sign. "You're going the wrong way!" Cam's hands grip the wheel and his shoulders are stiff.

"Don't worry. I know what I'm doing. The cab lurches forward as he hits the gas. I stare in horror as a car comes at us from the front. Cam flings the wheel to the right, throwing me across the back seat of the yellow. I hear a loud pop, then a crunch as he eases up on the gas and drives away. I sit up and look out the rear window. There is no sign of pursuit. The toothpick bounces up and down. "Sounds like he had a blowout." He pats the dashboard. "Those Fords can't top 40. I don't get to use third gear much. Who do you think they were?"

"I have no idea. But I'm betting a dollar to a doughnut Dolby is behind it." I fall back on the seat and exhale.

"Uh oh."

"What? Are they back?" I'm on alert again.

"No. She's overheating." He points to a wisp of steam flowing over the windshield as he pulls the car over to the curb. Cam hops out of the cab and pops the hood open. A minute later, he is back in the driver's seat. "Nothing blown, thankfully. Just running hot. I'll let her sit for a few minutes to cool off, and she'll be fine. I'll have to top off the water tonight." The toothpick twirls in his mouth. "I must've been going 50. I don't think I've ever done that."

48

"Maybe we should move. Leave the state." Tayla's voice is frantic. "If we leave, they'll stop hassling you."

I shake my head."I have a job here. I'd have to start over some place new. I don't want to do that."

"Look at you! Your face is a mess. You've been beaten and chased." She walks over to a drawer and pulls out a bandage.

"I'm healing. I'll be OK." I cringe as she pulls the old bandage off my chin.

"You won't heal if they keep pounding you."

"I'll try to avoid that."

She places her arms on my shoulders. "Do it for me. I don't need the paintings. I can paint new ones."

I look into her eyes. "How would it look if a reporter ran out because he was afraid? He'd be a coward. I'd never be able to get another job. Reporters are supposed to hunt and report the truth and the facts behind them, not run away when things get difficult."

"He'd be human. You're not a hero. You even told me you had quit worrying about who tried to kill you."

"You're right, I'm no hero." I wince. "And I did quit. I just don't like loose ends. We were followed–chased, but Cam was able to lose them. I need to know why and who wants me to stop doing whatever they fear."

Tayla pulls her hands off my shoulders. "You can't depend on the cabbie all the time. He got shoved into the trunk for gosh sakes. They'll come after you again. Just because you got rid of them once, doesn't mean they won't try again. Now they're angry."

"They were already angry. I promise I won't go out of my way to antagonize Dolby."

Tayla sighs, exasperated. "He's already antagonized. I didn't realize how thick-headed you can be." That hurt. "Please. You can find a new job. We can start a new life, a new family, together."

I stand, stunned, speechless. I hadn't thought about having a family. I'd just been content with having Tayla in my life. I was happy when I was with her. She was happy to be with me. I hadn't thought beyond that. Apparently she had. I'd never thought of myself as a father. I didn't remember mine, and I wasn't sure how I felt about kids since I didn't come across many. I felt detached from myself. I felt empty. I felt nothing. Things were moving too fast. "You—you're not—."

She stares at me. She laughs. "No, silly. I was just saying we could if we wanted to." I breathe a deep sigh of relief. I don't know if I want to have kids. Tayla continues, "Let's move. We could go to Jersey. It's not that far, and the ocean is there."

The thought of a family and settling down scared me. I admit it. A reporter doesn't get paid much. In D.C. there was always something to write about. In Jersey I'd be writing about trees and cows. I was better than that. Wasn't I?

I begin, "The world is crazy. We can't start a family. There's talk of war again. The way things are going it will be worse than the last one."

"I thought we were done with war." Tayla's eyes open wide.

I shrug. "I don't think we'll ever see the end of war. That's another reason for not bringing kids into the world now."

She looks at me with a puzzled expression. "What was the first one?"

I blink. "I meant a reason. But times are tough. I barely make enough to support myself."

Tayla stares at me. "Do—do you want me to leave?"

"No! Of course not! I want you in my life. I didn't mean you should leave. I'll make do."

Her expression softens. "I can always get a job too."

I fight the urge to scoff. "What kind of job?"

"They're opening up a new kind of store—department stores, they're called, all over. I could become a sales clerk. They're looking for a lot of women."

"I don't want you working."

Tayla's fists fly to her waist. "Don't you think I can work?"

"No. It's not that. But it's the man's job to support the woman."

She looks puzzled. "So you're saying it's the man's job to have a job?"

"Yes."

"If we can vote, we can have a job." Her voice is firm.

"But working isn't safe."

"Being a sales clerk is indoors. There's a security guard."

"You can't be a sales clerk."

"Have you ever been a sales clerk?"

"No."

"Do you want to be a sales clerk?"

"No."

"Then how do you know I can't be one?"

I was stumped. "Ok. You win. You can be anything you want to be." Tayla nods with satisfaction. "That doesn't mean you should be."

Tayla's expression slumps, then sets. Her voice rises. "Maybe this was a mistake."

"What?"

"Maybe it was a mistake moving in with you. I thought you were different. I thought you were a good guy. I guess I was wrong." She moves toward the bedroom. "You're just a schmuck. All you care about is yourself and how it affects you. You don't really care about me." She sobs. "You're—you're like Dolby." Tayla breaks down into tears, runs into the bedroom, and slams the door shut behind her.

I stare open-mouthed after her. Anger rises in me, or maybe frustration. I'm not sure which. I rush to the door and pull the knob, but she's locked the door. I pound on it. "Open up! Let me in!"

"Go away!" The muffled voice sobs back.

I hit the door again. "Don't be stupid. Let me in."

"Stupid? You think I'm stupid?"

I stare at the door. I hadn't thought things through again. "I didn't mean that. You're not stupid. Let me in and we can talk things over."

"If you didn't mean I was stupid, what did you mean?"

"I meant—I meant you were being childish." It came out before I realized what I'd said.

"Childish? Childish! Go away! I hate you! I never want to see you again!"

"I'm sorry. I really am. Let me in. I apologize." There was no response. I put my ear to the door and hear low sobbing. "Please. I didn't mean it. Forgive me!" The door remains shut. Frustrated, I curse myself and go for a walk to clear my mind and let my emotions cool.

49

The apartment door's open when I get back. She's left me, I think. My heart sinks. I go inside, then freeze. The apartment looks like a tornado had hit. Someone ransacked it. My breathing stops. "Tayla!", I scream as I run into the bedroom. It's empty. The closet door is flung open and our things are strewn over the floor. I scramble out into the hall and look down the steps. I hadn't passed anyone on the way up. They were gone. I take the steps three at a time and run outside. I sprint to the police station and collapse breathless against the sergeant's desk.

He comes around the desk and holds me up. "What happened? Are you OK?"

"They—they got her. I—I got home, and she was gone." My speech comes out in gasps.

"Who got her? Who did they get? Take a breath. Take it slow." I do as he says. My mind races to form words from my fears, and frantic guesses that come too fast. I take another breath.

"I got home. Tayla was gone. The house was ransacked. They got her."

"Tayla. Is that your girlfriend? Wife?"

I nod. "Girlfriend."

"Now who got her?"

"I don't—Dolby. Dolby got her."

The cop frowned. "Dolby. You mean Congressman Dolby?"

I nod. "He got her. I know he did."

The Sargeant's expression is skeptical. "Now why would a congressman grab your girlfriend?"

"She was his girlfriend until he hit her."

"But the Congressman has a wife."

My mind, breathing, and speech are now back to normal. My nerves are still on edge. "So? Lots of guys fool around."

"But he's a Congressman."

"He's still a guy."

"Are you sure you and—Tayla—you said that was her name, right? Are you sure you two didn't have a lover's spat, throw things around, and she up and left?"

"No!" I'm shocked. "Of course not. Well, we did have an argument, but I'd never throw things at her."

He looks doubtful. "You've been here before, you know."

"It's the truth. You wanted proof, well here's the proof. Go check out my place. You'll see."

"Ok. Ok. Calm down." The Sargeant calls over his shoulder. "Mike, grab your gear. We have a possible kidnapping."

Several minutes later, we are back at my apartment. The cops tell me to stay out in the hall while they go over the place. I am all jitters, waiting as they spend what seems like an hour inside the apartment. The Sargeant comes out.

"Well, what did I tell you?"

He pushes his cap back with a thumb. "Sorry I doubted you. There are definite signs of a struggle. What I want to know is where you the one that was struggling with her?"

"Of course not! We argued, but it never got physical."

"You said Congressman Dolby was involved. You realize that's a serious charge you're making?" I nod. "Ok. We'll send someone out to question him."

"He probably didn't do it himself. He hired some thugs. I think they're the ones that tried to kill me."

"Ok. We'll find out either way when we dust for prints. Stay out of the apartment until we can get a photographer to take pictures as evidence." He pauses. "And stay in the area in case we need you." I knew he actually meant if they had to arrest me. The other cop comes out and whispers to the sergeant. The sergeant turns back to me. "There's a knife with some blood on it under the bed. Know anything about it?"

I blanch. "No. What are you saying?"

"Not saying anything. I was asking."

"Tayla! Is she dead?"

"Calm down. There's no other blood except for the knife and some on the floor. If she's dead, she probably didn't die from a stab wound." I grimace. "You're free to go. But remember what I said, stay out of the apartment until we finish collecting the evidence."

50

The next day I have a visit from the Sargeant. "We checked out your story with the Congressman." The officer stands in my doorway. His expression is one of sour milk.

"And?" I prompt.

"Needless to say, he had an alibi. Also, he made it clear he'd sue you if you accused him again."

My stomach drops, but I'm not surprised by the response. It had been a long shot, and I already knew the Congressman wouldn't leave himself open to arrest. "Anything else? ," I ask.

"Yeah. I should take you in for wasting our time, but I'm just going to let you off with a warning." He pauses. "Don't screw around with us. We have actual crimes and criminals to deal with. We don't have time to go chasing after respectable citizens."

"Tayla! But what about Tayla?", I plead.

His tone softens. "Listen, she probably got fed up with you and went home to her mother. Give her some time to cool off."

"The blood–"

"Not enough to have killed someone. Take it from me. I think your imagination is running away from you." He sees the crestfallen expression on my face. "I'll tell you what I'll do. I'll put out an APB on your girl. I'll let you know if we find her." I'm despondent, but relieved that something would be done. The officer shakes his head as if to say, "Another crackpot," then leaves me looking after him.

A few moments later, I walk back into the apartment and make myself a pot of coffee. I know I'd pissed off Dolby. I was pissed as well. I'm going to see him caught and thrown behind bars for what he'd done to Tayla. The thought of the bloody knife still haunts me despite the Sargeant's reassurance. I glance at the green and browns of the landscape Tayla had given me that now hangs on the wall. I wish we could both escape into it.

51

I walk out of the building. I'm in a sweat and horrified at the thought of what might have happened to Tayla. If I hadn't gone out but instead worked through our argument, she would still be safe. If I hadn't been a dolt and said those stupid things, she'd still be safe and we'd be together. If I had agreed to move like she'd asked and not argued with her, she'd be safe. I go into a five-and-dime and plunk a coin into the pay phone.

Fifteen minutes later, I'm back in Cam's yellow on the way to the warehouse where I'd been held. The night is chilly; summer is ending. Dolby wasn't stupid enough to keep Tayla at his house. The warehouse would be the perfect place. It's out of the way and for the most part empty. We pull up to the loading area. The place is dark as I jump out of the cab and run up to the door. I tug and am not surprised the door's locked. I peer through the window, but can't see anything through the dirty glass. I swing an elbow and shards fly. I clear the jagged remains of the window and climb through into the cavernous blackness of the warehouse. My heart races as does my breath.

My eyes adjust, and I make out shapes. I run to the middle of the warehouse, expecting to find Tayla. There is no sign of her. I yell. "Tayla!" My voice rebounds off the stone walls. I'd been wrong. She wasn't here. Hope at finding her disappears and is replaced by a hollow emptiness inside of me. I climb out of the building and back into the cab.

"No luck." It's not a question. Cam's eyes peer at me in the rearview.

"No. She's not there."

"Back home?"

"Yeah—no. If she's not here and not at his house, she must be at the club. Get to the club."

52

I push and race past Jericho, who is again guarding the door, into the club. The fog of smoke hits me in the face, and I pause to look around. The band is playing some loud jazz. I think it's called the "Charleston" and most of the patrons are gyrating wildly on the dance floor. I fight my way to the bar.

"The usual?" Moe takes a break from watching the dancing to ask me.

"Where is she?"

"Who?"

"Tayla."

The bartender stares at me as if I'm insane. "Tayla? I haven't seen her since the day you got dumped in the river."

"Don't lie. She has to be here. She's in the back room. I know it."

He focuses on me. There is concern in his voice. "Did something happen to Tayla? Is she OK?"

I grab him by his collar. "Don't act dumb. You know your goons kidnapped her and stabbed her."

Moe's jaw drops in shock. "Stabbed? Who stabbed her? When? Where?"

"You had something to do with all of this–me–Tayla–everything!"

He raises his hands in surrender. "Honest. I didn't do it. I—I have no idea what you're talking about."

I study his face. The shock and concern are palpable. I drop his collar. "Dolby's goons got her while I was out of our apartment."

Moe's face contorts in pain. "She's living with you? What's this about her being stabbed?"

"The cops found a bloody knife."

"Shit."

"Where is she?" I catch sight of the back room door. "She's in there, isn't she?" I push my way through the crowd to the door.

"She's not there. Stop! You can't go in there." Moe's yell is drowned out by the laughter, noise, and music.

I push a younger man out of the way in my rush to the door. He stands his ground and pushes back. He stares at me defiance or maybe hatred on his face. I shove him and move toward the door. I'm jerked back and spun around by my shoulder. A fist flies toward my already hammered face. I duck and throw a punch. I need to get to Tayla. I feel him give under the punch to his stomach. His breath is forced out of his lungs, and his spit hits my face. Rage hits me and I swing again. This time I strike his chin and send him sprawling. Shouts and yells break out. A woman screams. I continue to fight my way through the ensuing bedlam. An old gent who is trying to chat up a young babe leans against the door. "Excuse me," I yell as I shove him out of the way. He stumbles to the floor. The babe gasps and rushes to his side. I reach for the knob of the office. A hand grabs my shoulder—the guy I had knocked out. I'm spun around. My arm goes into motion. Before my fist connects, I'm wrapped up in a bear hug and manhandled through the crowd. I'm thrown out the door to the pavement. I hear a cheer from those inside the club.

Jericho towers over me. All my wounds and bruises cry out. I'm flat on my back. "What the hell do you think you're doing? You know the rules."

"I—" I moan. "I need to help, Tayla."

"I don't care if you have to help the Pope himself. Keep out if you know what's good for you."

"I'm sorry. I just want to help Tayla." I struggle to get up. He grabs me by the arm and pulls me upright in a single motion.

"You should know better," he growls as he brushes my jacket off with his hands. His left hand wears the ring. "Nothing personal. You're a good kid. But this is a business. No cops. No Feds. No guns. No trouble. You broke the rule."

"But—she's in there. I know it. I have to save her. She's hurt."

Jericho blocks the door. "Sorry. You don't want to make more trouble."

I take a step forward. He folds his arms over his chest. His legs are spread. I stop. I turn around and walk down the alley to the street. I curse. I've run out of options. I turn the corner when something hits the back of my head.

53

"You really don't learn, do you?" I hear the voice through a thick fog as I come to. "You're in over your head. Stop butting in where you don't belong. You're going to mess things up. This is your last warning. Next time you won't be so lucky." I fight through the haze to focus. The street is empty. I stagger to my feet. My head throbs. Old wounds wake up and add to the pain. My vision blurs. I pass out again.

54

I wake up in a hospital bed. Disoriented, I look around. How did I get here? The memory of last night flows back into my addled brain. Tayla! I pull my legs over the edge of the bed and stand. The world spins and I drop back down. I let the blood move back into my head and then I stand slowly and put on my clothes. I crack open the door of the hospital room and peek out. The hallway is clear, so I move as quickly as my condition allows. My brain feels as if it bounces with each step that I take, and my head feels as if it's been stabbed with a hot poker. My vision blurs then clears, then blurs again. I hear voices. I stop. I don't want anyone stopping me just because I'd been blind-sided. I have to find Tayla. The voices pass without entering the hallway. I continue to the stairwell, but before I reach it a man in a white coat pulls the door open and stops when he sees me. "Mr. Cook? What are you doing out of your bed? You have a serious concussion. You need to get back in bed and stay there." I try to push him out of my way, but fail. My strength is gone, and he easily grabs me by the elbow and leads me back to my room. I drop back onto the bed, exhausted. "That's good. Now just relax and heal." He pulls my eyelids apart and stares into my left eye. "Still dilated. Is your vision blurred?" I nod. He moves his finger around, tracking my eyes. "Now where do you think you were going?"

"I—I have to find Tayla."

"That can wait. You need to take care of yourself" He pulls up a clipboard. "You were here last week, weren't you? You went through quite a beating then: bruises, cuts, contusions. Now this? Do you want to talk about it?" The doctor looks at me over the board.

"No. It's personal."

"Well, if you do, I'm here to listen. In the meantime, take it easy, and maybe you can be out of here tomorrow. I'll check in on you then." He replaces the clipboard, gives a pat on my leg, then leaves. Cam enters as the doctor exits.

"You're awake. I just stopped in to see how you're doing, boss."

"I'll survive. How'd'you know I was here?"

"Who do you think dragged your sorry carcass here?"

"You did?"

"Who else? When you didn't come back to the cab after I dropped you off, I went looking for you. I found you face down on the sidewalk. I got you into the cab and rushed you over here."

"I owe you one."

"That's two, boss. The first one was when they locked me in the trunk. Remember?"

I grunt an acknowledgement as I get out of the bed. "Come on. Help me get out of this joint. I need to find Tayla."

Cam's toothpick stops moving. "Are you serious? You were just clobbered and the docs say you have a concussion. You're in no shape to do anything."

I move to the door. I'm forgetting something, something important, but my head throbs and I can't concentrate. I focus on getting out. "Don't argue. I'll survive. Get me out of here before the jailers grab me again."

Cam stands a moment, considering."Ok, you owe me three." We leave the hospital without being stopped. We enter the cab when Cam says, "Oh, I filed a police report about the attack."

I fall back onto the seat. I'm dizzy and weak. I mumble. "Why did you do that?"

"I figured the third time's a charm." Cam chuckles as he starts the engine and the cab rolls onto the street. "The cop said to tell you they'll get a statement from you tomorrow. They also said to tell you you can go back to your place. They're done with getting what they need."

"Thanks. Did they tell you if they found anything?"

"Nope. Sorry."

"Take me back to the club. I need to find Tayla."

Cam stares at me in the mirror. "No way. I'm taking you home. You need to heal up. Besides, I heard about the ruckus you made. They probably won't let you back in."

I struggle to sit upright. "I have to go back. She's there. She needs me."

"You're in no shape. Take it from me. You aren't much help to anyone in the shape you're in."

A wave of dizziness washes over me and I fall back onto the seat. "Maybe you're right."

55

I climb the steps up to my apartment to find the door is unlocked. The cops must've forgotten to lock it when they were done. I push the door open and go in. I move to the kitchen to get some food and stop in my tracks. Dolby sits in a chair in the main room amid the mess left by Tayla's abduction. In an instant, my mind focuses.

"What do you want? What did you do with Tayla?". I move toward him, my hands clench into fists as I do. Dolby doesn't flinch. Instead, he points to another chair.

"Sit down. I just want to talk to you."

"What did you do with Tayla? If you killed her—"

"Sit down." The Congressman's voice is firm. "I haven't killed her." My vision blurs again. I sit.

"Where is she?" I mumble. My head feels like it's been cracked open by a sledgehammer.

His voice becomes quiet. "She's safe. For now."

"What do you want?"

"Want? From you? Nothing."

"Nothing?"

"Well, nothing but a promise."

I try to focus again, but I struggle to stay conscious. "What promise?"

"That you'll stop meddling in my affairs."

"I thought you said you weren't the owner of the club."

Dolby spreads his hands. "I'm not." I'm in too much pain to discern whether the scum is telling the truth. "Let's just say I have my own interests there."

I don't understand. "What about Tayla? If I promise, will you set her free?"

"No. She ran out on me." His voice drips hate and anger. "She ran out on me. After I set her up in her own place. After I promoted her. I made her mine." He stands in rage. "She threw it all away." Dolby takes a breath and sits, once again calm. "She betrayed everything I did. She has to pay."

My mind scrambles to form some sort of plan. "What about your wife?"

"What about her? She has nothing to do with this and if she ever finds out, I'll know where the information came from. Now promise. I'll take your word."

"No. Not unless you let Tayla go."

He cocks his head. "You really love her, don't you?"

"Of course I do. She's—she's all I have."

The Congressman sighs. "Well, you don't have much then, do you?"

I stumble to stand and move at the man in the chair. With a single hand, he pushes me aside into the kitchen counter. Whimpering, I slump to the ground.

Dolby moves to the door of the apartment. He turns back to me. "I'll take that as a no."

56

I push myself off the floor and stagger to the chair. The pain in my side tells me I won't be moving fast for a while. At least my face is healing. I'm dizzy, a result of the concussion, no doubt. I could use a shot of whiskey. I sit and feel sorry for myself. I sit a long time. Tayla had been right. We should have moved when we had the chance. Now it's too late. If I hadn't bumbled into Dolby's mess, we would both be healthy and happy.

I stumble to the kitchen and make a cup of coffee. As I drop into a chair, I feel I'm forgetting something important, but I still can't focus. I look at the apartment, that is still in tatters. Tayla's belongings are strewn about and mixed with my own. I have to find her. I'd gotten her into this mess; I had to get her out. If nothing else, Dolby's visit confirmed he had her. I'm sure she's being held in the club. I consider going back to the cops, but Cam had told me they would be paying me a visit tomorrow, anyway. That could wait. I sip the coffee and stare out the window at the street. There isn't much traffic and only a few people walk by. I have to get into the back room when the club isn't open and busy. Now is the perfect time. I throw the rest of the coffee into the sink and walk past Tayla's painting feeling as green as the trees in it.

57

An hour later I'm sitting in Cam's cab, which is parked on the street near the club. "Are you sure you're up to this? I told you, you need to rest up. Maybe you should quit while you're ahead." The toothpick doesn't move.

"I need to get her. She's hurt. And Dolby threatened to do more." The pain in my head has receded. The one in my side is still there. "She's in the back room. I just know it."

"Well, the joint is closed. Are you going to break in? The cops will get you if they find out."

"I have no choice." I swing the door open and step out of the cab. The alley is clear as I walk toward the entrance to the club.

"Wait up." Cam jogs up to me.

"What?"

"Why are you going in the front door?" I stop not understanding. I'm not thinking straight. "There's a door to the back room I saw when I was watching the tree house. Wouldn't that be easier?" He holds up a screwdriver. "You'll need this."

I lead the way around to the back of the club. The courtyard is empty apart from a couple of chairs stacked by the wall, extras that had been brought in for the overflow last night. I walk to the door and a wave of dizziness causes me to stumble. Cam catches me. "You OK? You really need to get back to the hospital."

I force myself to focus. "I'm fine. Just a little dizzy." I take the screwdriver and struggle to clear my vision enough to jimmy the door open.

"Well, we've just broken the law. Breaking and entering."

"We haven't gone in yet." Cam grunts. I push the door open and enter the room. Cam waits outside. The only light comes from the open door and the room is as I remember seeing it. Tayla is not there. I curse.

"Is she here?" Cam looks into the room.

"No. Damn! I was sure she was." I use the screwdriver to pry the top off of one of the cases that is stacked along the walls.

"What are you doing?"

"Seeing if I'm right about Dolby and what I think is whiskey. If he's bringing in whiskey in addition to gin, he's probably selling it to the Army to help with the flu we just got through. The Army gives bootleggers a break." I peer at the bottle in my hand. "The colored glass makes it hard to tell if it's whisky," I continue. I pull a bottle out and hold it up to the light streaming in from the outside. The liquid is clear. It might be whiskey. I hear muffled voices inside the club, but can't make out what they're saying. I put the lid back onto the crate. "Let's get out of here."

"Good idea."

We shut the door and get back to the cab. Cam looks at me in the mirror. "That whiskey?"

"I don't know. This glass is too dark to know. I'll have to open the bottle to find out. That's why I took it."

"Where to?"

"Back to my place. I'm about to fall over."

58

I pull the cork out of the bottle and pour some of the clear liquid into a glass, then sniff it. It's gin. I was certain it was going to be whiskey. I was wrong about Tayla being in the club. I was wrong about the whiskey. I hadn't linked Dolby to the warehouse. I hadn't linked him to the club. I hadn't linked him to bootlegging. I stare down at the glass, shrug, and down the liquid. It burns my throat. I feel better. The pain is still there, but it's manageable. I pour another shot and sit down at the kitchen table to plan my next move. I have to find Tayla. If she isn't in the warehouse or the club, then Dolby had her at his home. That would be harder to get into than the club. It would also be harder to get out. I swirl the gin in the glass and take another sip. It isn't very good, but it's a far cry from the worst I'd had in my life.

I have to get inside the Congressman's home. It's large and it will take time to search all the rooms. It would be impossible to do that with anyone there. I doubt the servants would leave the house unattended. Maybe I could talk the one that answered the door into helping me. He seemed amenable to me and didn't appear to like Dolby very much. I consider asking Cam to help, but there is no need to involve him in any more illegal activity. I take another sip.

Once I found her, we'd go somewhere safe. She wanted to go to Jersey. It could be worse. Who knows, I might even find a job on a small paper. That reminded me. I pick up the phone and check in with my editor. A couple of minutes later, I hang up. He wants me to cover a dedication of some sort of fountain. I grimace and take another sip. At least I had a plan.

The sun is setting so I can't do anything else today. I ache. I hurt. I hate it. I get up and get a couple of Bayer from the medicine cabinet in the bathroom. I down them with the rest of the glass, drop on the bed, and am out.

59

I wake up the next morning feeling better. Not perfect, just better. The pain in my head is a dull throb. My side still hurts, but I'll live. My face is less puffy and I look human; again not perfect, just better. I spend the morning cleaning up the mess left by whoever had grabbed Tayla. Picking up her belongings hurts both physically and emotionally. Her scent lingers on her things. Even though my heart feels like it has been crushed: I miss her. I'm moving slow. I'm afraid of what I might discover when I find her. I'd screwed up–I had done this to her. She was the only dame I'd ever really loved. She was the only one I'd ever cared about emotionally. Pangs of regret stab through my heart. A month ago I hadn't known her. Now I can't imagine being alive earlier than a month ago. I curse because I know I'm procrastinating. I call a cab, making sure it isn't Cam who responds. A short while later, I walk up the path to the mansion. The Congressman would be busy on Capitol Hill today, or so the paper said. I knock. The servant opens the door and recognizes me. "The Congressman is out."

"That's OK. I want to talk to you."

The servant remains straight-faced. "About, sir?"

"About whether you've seen Tayla Bourke? I mean in the past few days."

"I can't say I have, sir."

That sounded non-committal. "I mean, is she here? Now?"

"No, sir."

"Was she here in the past few days?"

"No, sir. I haven't seen Miss. Bourke in the last week."

"Oh." I'm crestfallen. I'd hoped he could shed some light on where she might be. "Is there any place she could be in the house without you knowing about it?" A good reporter asks probing questions. I'm not a good reporter.

The servant looks at me, puzzled. "No, sir. I don't believe so. May I ask what this is regarding?"

"Tayla has been abducted."

The man drops his facade but regains it a moment later. "I'm sorry to hear that, sir. She seemed a nice person, sir."

I nod. "I think the Congressman is connected."

"To her abduction?" Shock is now plain on his face.

"I think so. I need to find her."

He shakes his head. "I'm sorry, sir. If she were here, I would let you know."

"Thank you. I guess I need to look elsewhere."

"My pleasure, sir. I'm—perturbed Miss Tayla is gone and the possibility the Congressman is involved."

"Me too."

60

I walk out to the street and stop to look back at the imposing stone building. I can't be wrong again. I turn the corner off of O Street and push through the hedges that surround the home. I'm at the back of the structure. There's a second path that leads to a door. It's locked. I try several windows and am rewarded by one that opens. I crawl through to enter the house and find I'm in some sort of pantry or larder. The sunlight that streams through the window lights the room. I peek into a hallway and see there is nothing fancy in this part of the home. I'm in the servant's section of the house. Tayla wouldn't be here. It would be too busy, and Dolby would be too easily found out. I move down the main hall. There is no sign of any servants, and I had only seen the man who answered the door. I open another door, which takes me to the main dining room. I'm no longer in the servant's area. Moving across the room to a door that stands open, I almost walk in on an old woman toiling over a large pot in the kitchen. The smell of stew hits me full in the face and my stomach growls. I back away, lucky she hadn't heard it. The other rooms on the lower floor are empty.

I'd never amount to much if the money spent here was any sign. The opulence I'd seen in Dolby's office extends throughout the non-servant's area of the house. I stop as I climb up the steps to the living area. My vision blurs and grows dark. I sit down on the top step and hold my head between my knees. Cam was right. I should go to the hospital and get better, but first I have to get Tayla. I get up and search the rooms on the top floor, one by one. They are empty apart from one. When I enter, a scream stuns me. A woman stands in the bedroom clutching a dress in front of her. I rush out and trip down the steps. I crawl out of the window in the servant's area just as the manservent runs into the room. I'm not sure he has seen me. Panting, I scramble through the hedges and down the street as shouts and yells come from behind. I round the corner and collapse against a wall. My head pounds. I gasp for air and feel like throwing up. I wait for the nausea to pass, hail a yellow, then go home.

61

The next evening, I climb out of a cab and walk up the alley to the club. Jericho Waldroup sees me and growls, "You again. You here to cause more problems?" Memory of the night when I was tossed out flashes back to me. That's what I'd forgotten. He wore the ring—a ring like the one the person who had dumped me in the river wore. My brain isn't thinking straight. I should have remembered. "Well? Are you going to stand there like a statue?"

I shake my head and focus. "No. I just need a drink."

Jericho considers a moment. "Well I haven't been told to keep you out, so you know the rules. No Feds, no cops, no guns. No trouble. Especially no trouble. Got it?"

"Got it." He pats me down.

"Nice ring."

"Huh?" He glances at his hand.

"I hear a lot of government guys wear one like that."

He peers at me. I squirm under the scrutiny. "Where'd you hear that?"

"I'm a reporter, remember?"

"Yeah. It's just a ring." He's lying.

"Where'd you get it? I'd like to get one like that. Unless, of course, it's a government thing."

"It was a present." He's still lying.

"Oh. Never mind then. Have a good night." I walk into the club. I feel Waldroup's gaze on my back. My nerves are on edge, not because I'm going in but because of the bouncer's lies. I wonder what I've walked into.

62

It's still early, and the joint hasn't filled yet. A few guys are hanging around the bar with Moe. He spots me from across the room and his expression sets to a hard sour frown. I greet him. "How's it going?"

"You again? I don't need trouble in this place. You better leave before I have Jericho toss you out on your ear."

I raise a hand. "I'm only here for a drink. Promise. I'm in no shape to cause any problems."

He looks at me for a long half minute, then pours a glass. "Did they find Tayla?" There is concern in his voice.

"No. Sorry."

He passes the gin over to me. "Enjoy. Just don't look for trouble."

"I never do, but it always seems to find me." I take the glass and move to an empty corner table. The band hasn't even set up yet. There are at least two people with that ring. Jericho has one. One of the two thugs who had roughed me up has the other. Why would the Feds want to dump me in the river? My brain still isn't thinking clearly and my head still throbs, but my vision has stabilized. Maybe the concussion is healing. I take a swig of the gin. It's awful. I go back to the bar.

"This is swill." I place the glass in front of Moe. "You cutting it with something?"

Moe looks perplexed as he shakes his head. He picks up the glass and takes a sip. His face contorts. "You're right. It must be a bad bottle. I'll get a fresh one from the back." He disappears into the back room. I can't see if Dolby is there, but I hear Moe arguing with whoever is there. He comes out a minute later with a fresh bottle. He dumps the contents of my glass and refills it from the new bottle. "Sorry about that. This should be better."

I take a sip and nod. "The owner's in?"

"No."

"Who were you arguing with then?"

Moe's stare is stern. "You looking for trouble?"

"No. No. I was just wondering." I take the glass and hurry back to the table before Moe has me tossed into the alley. I sit and sip. An hour passes as I watch the place fill. The band comes out and starts setting up as I look around the room. Something is different. The walls are bare. The art exhibit is gone. Perplexed, I go back to Moe. "What happened to the art?"

"The show's over." He hands an elderly woman dressed to the nines a glass of "water".

"I figured that. But what happens to the art itself?"

Moe shrugs. "I guess it goes back to the artists. It's not up to me. I just serve drinks." He takes an order from a young couple. That's a hint the conversation with me is at an end. I return to my table. The place isn't as busy as it had been the last few nights, and the band sounds like it's just going through the motions. No one is dancing. It's Monday. I'm not sure what I'm doing there as I sit and nurse my drink throughout the night. I've run out of ideas. I glance at the clock behind the bar. It's almost closing time—one in the morning. I have to discover where Dolby is holding Tayla and I have to catch him with the evidence. I stare into the glass and groan. I don't want to get roughed up again. I've had enough.

"Last call!" Moe's voice yells from behind the bar. The band plays their last number, a slow dance, but no one dances. I get up and move to the exit. Jericho is leaning against the wall and having a smoke. He nods as I move past. He has a ring. He's the one. I'm certain. I quicken my pace. I knew who, I still don't know why.

63

I turn the corner and flinch, expecting to be clobbered again. But no one is there. Moe's yellow isn't there either. He probably had a fare and didn't feel like losing it while waiting for me. I stand on the sidewalk, deciding whether I should call another cab or wait for Moe to come back. I decide to wait. A few people come out of the alley and pass by me. I brace myself for an attack each time anyone does. I'm tired. I'm jumpy and I'm second guessing my decision to wait.

I walk. The night's dark so I decide not to take any chances and stop under a street lamp. A chill breeze hits the back of my neck. I pull my collar up. It's going to be a cold winter. I'm tired. My body and head feel sluggish, but the pain has receded. I don't know whether I'm healing or feeling the effects of the alcohol. I don't care. A pair of headlights turns onto the street. The car's beams light up the area in front of it into the grays and blacks of the city. The car pulls up to the curb next to me and I see the silhouette of Cam's head and toothpick. I slide into the back seat.

"Sorry I'm late. I had a couple of fares on the other side of town."

"Good tippers?"

"Nothing to write home about. A bunch of drunk guys who had a party to go to. They were already partying when I picked them up." Cam glances into the mirror as he steers the car back onto the street. "So how'd it go?" The light of the dash casts a ghoulish glow over his face.

"It didn't."

"Sounds like you've hit a wall."

"Yeah. The only thing I got out of tonight is they have taken the art exhibit down. No Tayla as far as I could tell."

"You're shooting snake eyes."

"It seems that way."

"What's the plan?"

"I wish I knew. I'm out of ideas. The one thing I'm certain of is Dolby has her. I need to either find her or take him out of the picture."

Cam's eyebrows shoot up in the mirror. "You ain't thinking of killing him, are you?"

"No. Of course not." I'm as shocked as he is. "I just meant if I could get the cops to bust him we might find out where he's stashed Tayla."

"He's a Congressman. He's probably got lawyers for his lawyers. Even if you could get the cops to bust him, he'd be out in no time. He'd know who put them on his scent—you." Cam is right, of course. "He'd come down on you twice as hard." For an instant, I want to ask Cam for his gun. It seems the only way to end this was to end Dolby. I sigh. I'm thinking crazy. "How're you feelin'?" Cam's question brings my focus back to reality.

"Ok, I guess. The gin helps."

"Sounds like the cure is worse than the cause. Me, I don't touch the stuff. There's a reason they call it rock gut. Before the dry times gin was safe. Now, you don't know what you're gettin'." I grunt. As long as it helps the pain, I think. Cam continues, "It's like smokin'. Everyone does it, but me. Something that good can't be good for you, get what I mean?" I'm not sure about the last but agree about the smoking. I decide to switch topics.

"So what do you do when you're not carrying fares?"

"Me? I work. I have to. My mom's getting up in years and her health ain't so good. Lots of bills. She lives with me. Ninety-seven and still riding my tail. God bless her. She doesn't move as fast as she did. Docs say it's her ticker."

"Sorry to hear."

"It's OK. We all have to go sometime. It's just a matter of how you choose to go."

"What do you do for fun?"

"I don't have time for fun. When I was a kid, I wanted to grow up and be a ballplayer–and a cowboy. Then I grew up and discovered you need money to get anywhere. I did bit jobs then hired on with Yellow. The pay is good and the hours don't kill me." The cab pulls up in front of my building. "Here you go. Are you going to need me tomorrow?"

"Yeah. Tomorrow around lunch."

64

Nightmares of Tayla screaming and blood kept me from getting a full night's sleep. I got up tired, aching, and groggy. I grabbed a cold shower that woke me and soothed some of the pain–mental and physical. My head was clear for a change. Hot coffee returned my focus, and I felt better than I'd had in days. Maybe today would be when the mess would turn around. I knew I had to get Dolby to tell me where Tayla was, and I wasn't going to find her any other way. The problem was I had no idea how to do it. I looked at the clock. I had a couple of hours before Cam showed up, so I called into the office. They still wanted me to cover the fountain dedication. It was meaningless to me. I thought I was a decent reporter, but I'd been fooling myself. I covered art, dog shows, and fountain dedications. I'd covered nothing worthwhile. I threw a couple of eggs into the fry pan and cooked breakfast, which I ate but didn't taste. I had screwed up big time. I had to make it right for her. I thought and chewed. I gave Cam a call and postponed having him come until that evening. By the time Cam honked outside, I knew what I had to do.

65

"You're crazy." Cam's toothpick agrees. "You're asking to be arrested—or worse."

"I don't have any other choice."

Cam's head shakes from side to side. "I don't like it. You're looking for trouble. The Congressman won't be easy."

"Never mind. It's my problem. Now lets get to the club." The cab pulls out into traffic. A short time later, we arrive.

"How do you know he's even in? You've never seen him here."

"I don't. But he has to show up if he's the owner. I just have to wait until he does." I sigh. "And if he doesn't show up, I may have to do something more drastic."

"Want me to come with you?" Cam taps the glove compartment. The cab sits by the alley.

"No. I want you to wait here. The club won't open for a couple of hours. That will give me time to get set."

"I don't know. It doesn't sound smart."

I flinch. "It will work. All I have to do is make him think I've written a piece exposing him. If he doesn't free Tayla, I'll publish it."

"Isn't that like blackmail?"

"He's a crook and a scum. I don't think blackmailing someone like that matters. He needs to be brought to justice. Tayla needs to be freed. That's all I care about. I've screwed up enough. I need to do this—otherwise I'm just a failure."

"He'll just call the goons on you and you'll disappear. You're not a failure. Sure you've been roughed up, but you have done nothing that the cops can't fix."

"They're not doing anything. Don't you get it?" I'm getting angry. "I'm nobody to them. They need proof. I don't want Tayla's body to be that proof. I need to do this for her. I need to do this for me." I get out of the cab before Cam can talk me out of what I have to do.

66

I have to get inside from the back of the club before it opens for the
night. I'd tried the direct way, and that hadn't worked. I have to get
Dolby alone. I pull the door and see they had replaced the lock. The
door won't budge. I hadn't brought anything with which to jimmy the
door. Cursing, I pick up a rock and smash it against the lock. The only
thing I do is to cause a lot of noise that I don't need. I toss the rock
aside. My heart pounds and for an instant I consider getting Cam's
gun and shooting the lock, but just as quickly discount the idea. I move
to the window, which is open a crack, but that doesn't help me get
through the bars. My plan is falling apart even before it starts. The
sound of a truck causes me to scamper around the corner of the
building and plant myself against the bricks. I'm panting as I hear the
truck brake to a stop and a few moments later Moe's voice. He orders
someone to unload the gin. It's another delivery. I hug the wall tighter
as the sound of steps comes my way, then breathe a sigh of relief when
I hear Moe unlock the door. I wait as the men make several trips
between the truck and the office. After what seems an eternity, I hear
the door close and the van start up. A moment later, the sound of it
driving off fades in the distance. I wait another couple of minutes to
make sure it's gone and move back to the courtyard. The sun is setting;
the air is chilly, dark clouds are gathering, and I'm running out of time.
The club would be open soon and I won't be able to get inside without
attracting attention. I try the door again, and this time it swings open.
It had been closed but not locked. I silently thank the powers that be
and my luck. I enter, closing the door behind me.

67

The room is dark, but I remember where the desk is. I go to it and sit down, then pull a box of matches from my pocket and light one. I pull the drawer open and rummage through the contents. I'm not sure what I'm looking for, just something that would incriminate the Congressman. The drawer holds nothing worthwhile. I wave the match out and curse. Dolby's too clever to keep anything here. I place my elbows on the blotter that's on the desk and stare at the thin slit of light under the door to the rest of the club. Where would he keep information that was safe from prying eyes but readily available? I light another match and glance around the room. The only other things in it are the wooden cases. He wouldn't hide anything in them. I look down at the desk again. I wonder. I flip the blotter over. Nothing. I'd hoped to find something written on the back. It was a piece of cardboard that has a pocket on either end into which blotting paper could be inserted. The cardboard kept ink from penetrating to the desk. The blotting paper is thicker than normal. I pull it out and am rewarded by a sheet of paper under it. The match burns down to my fingers and I yelp as the flame singes them. I light another and look at the paper I'd found. Names are handwritten on it. I don't know what they mean even though I recognize several of the names as people in government.

Voices in the club grab my attention. I replace the sheet and the blotter. I want to confront Dolby, but I hadn't thought things through again. If he finds me in the club after I'd broken in, I wouldn't see tomorrow. The voices grow louder and are moving toward me. I scamper out the back door. I run as fast as I can back to the cab, then slump into the back seat, out of breath. Cam looks at me in surprise and relief. "What happened? You change your mind?"

My breath slows. "No. I just changed the plan. I need a more direct approach. I don't know what I was thinking. I'm not built for spying and burglary."

"So what's the new plan?"

"I don't know. But I need to think things through. I discovered one thing. Too bad I don't know what it means."

"Home?"

"No. I need to get back in there and confront Dolby. I just need to do it in public, not in the back room. There have to be witnesses. Even if he kills me there have to be witnesses."

"You planning on getting killed, boss?"

"No. Not if I can help it. I don't even want to get beat up again. I've had enough. I just want this over and done. I just want to get back to a nice safe life of a reporter covering fluff." I look at my watch. "The club should be opening in a couple of minutes" I climb out of the cab. "Stay here. If I'm not out in an hour send in the cavalry."

"Want me to come along? In case you need help?"

"No. I may need to get out quick."

"Sure thing, boss."

68

I notice Jericho Waldroup isn't manning the door this evening, or it's still too early. I'd hoped I might be able to convince him into pulling me out of trouble if I ran into it. That was a long shot, but it was worth a try. He's gone and I'm alone. I enter the club's main entrance and I find the place empty, and Moe is just setting up. He nods when he sees me coming into the place. I walk up to him. "How's it going?"

"You're here early. We're not open yet. Come back later—or not."

"Where's Jericho tonight?"

"He's busy. Did you want to talk to him about something?"

"No, I was just wondering. I really want to talk to the boss."

"You never give up, do you?"

I shrug. "I try."

"Any word about Tayla?"

"No. I'm still looking for her."

"Poor kid. I wonder what happened to her." There's genuine concern in his voice and something I can't put my finger on.

"That's what I want to talk to the owner about. Is he in?" I nod at the back room.

"I'll check. I need to get some bottles, anyway." Moe enters the back room and shuts the door behind him. I glance around the room. It's still empty. I'm the only one there. I'd have to wait because I need witnesses. For a moment I consider leaving before I jump into the deep end, but then Moe returns carrying a couple of bottles. He returns to the bar but says nothing. I watch him open one of the bottles and pour a glass.

I raise an eyebrow. "I didn't order a drink."

"It's on the house." I reach for the drink. He takes the glass before I can. "It's for the house—me. Did you want one?"

"Sure."

Moe nods and pours another. "Bottoms up." I down the glass in a single shot. I reach for my wallet. He interrupts me. "That one's on me."

"Thanks. Why are you being so friendly, all of a sudden?"

He tilts his head at the back room. "The boss will see you." My eyebrows shoot up. "You asked?"

Moe shrugs. "I got tired of having you bugging me. Besides, you're trying to help Tayla." The way he said the last was wistful. He loved her.

I put the glass back on the bar. "Thanks. She's a good kid." I open the door and walk in.

69

The room is as I'd left it minutes ago, except that Dolby sits behind the desk. Jericho stands in front of it. I hesitate and turn to leave. Dolby dismisses the bouncer with a wave of his hand and points to a chair that wasn't in the room when I'd searched it. "Make sure we're not disturbed." Dolby turns to me. "Have a seat." I look at Jericho as he passes me, but he doesn't read my desire for him to stay.

"I can see you're busy. I can come back later." My nerve has run out on me.

"Have a seat." My legs turn to jelly, and I drop into the chair. "You really are annoying, aren't you? You don't seem to take hints or warnings. You even don't respond to me threatening Tayla." Dolby sighs. "Now what am I going to do with you?"

"Is she still alive?" My heart leaps.

"Of course. I had hoped my threats would dissuade you from nosing around in my business, but it appears that hasn't worked. Maybe I should get rid of her after all."

"Where is she?" I stand up.

"Sit down." His growl forces me back down. "I have a simple question. I want a simple answer. I want the truth. Why are you sticking your nose where it doesn't belong? Is it because you're writing a story?"

"Yes." It's mostly a lie.

"As I thought. So the question is, what do you think you have found out?" He steeples his fingers on the blotter. I make a concerted effort not to stare at it. "I'm a Congressman, I can make your life miserable. You may as well tell me what you've found." He pours a shot of gin from a bottle on the desk. "Want one?" I shake my head. "So what do you think you know?"

"I don't know anything."

"Now now. Don't be that way. We're all friends here."

"I—I was trying to find Tayla. That's all I care about."

"I see." He stands up and walks over to a stack of crates. "How chivalrously noble of you." He picks an object off of the crate.

"That's the truth. I just want to get Tayla back."

"I wish I could believe that. Really, I do. It would make things so much easier." Dolby walks toward me. My blood rushes from my head. I see what he's carrying. It's a screwdriver—Moe's screwdriver that I had used the first night I had broken into the room and crates. I had left it behind. I curse silently.

"I just want to save her. You—you threatened to kill her." I'm babbling. I'm sweating.

The Congressman stands in front of me. He holds up the screwdriver. "This wouldn't be yours by chance, would it?"

I shake my head. "No—I've never seen it before in my life."

"Really? Well, I think you're lying." He plays with the screwdriver. "No one else has been buzzing around here–and this isn't mine." I move to push him away to escape, but he moves faster than I thought was possible. The screwdriver swings down and plunges into my thigh. I scream as the pain rips through my leg and into my brain. My vision blurs and I fight to stay conscious. Blood spurts out around the screwdriver that has pinned me to the chair. My mind goes blank to everything but the pain. "Oh, don't worry about upsetting anyone in the club. I guessed you might try to break in and snoop around. I've closed the club for the night so we can have our little chat in private." He grabs me by my collar and pulls me forward. "Now why don't you tell me what you've found out." Tears form from the pain. I struggle to focus. I have to get out. "Tell me," he snarls.

I have to give him something. Anything. "I—I know you scam the artists."

"Is that all?" He throws me back against the chair. He leans in and jiggles the screwdriver. Blood pools on the floor. I scream again. My vision fades. I shake my head to stay alert. I pant. I can't think. It's all I can do to stay conscious. "You—you run gin—and whiskey." Dolby sits behind the desk again. I wipe the tears from my eyes with an arm so I can see. The pain beings to fade. My leg goes numb. I try to slow my wild breathing, but I have no control over the beating of my heart. I avoid looking at my leg so I don't pass out.

"See? That wasn't so hard, was it? Well, well, well. You really have been a busy little bee." He leans forward on the desk. "Now, what am I going to do with you? Hm?" I'm too busy dealing with the pain and trying to stay alert to answer. "Well, I can't let you go free now, can I? After all, I can't let you write your story. It wouldn't do to have the world know of my—hobbies."

"It's—written." I manage to utter through the pain. Dolby sits up startled. "I—I wrote it. I was going to give it to my editor tomorrow."

"You wouldn't be lying to me now, would you? After all, we're friends."

"It's written—I just need to send it in." I'm lying. It's the only thing I can come up with. "They'll find it if I disappear."

Dolby sits behind the desk. He's silent for a long minute, deep in thought. "We can't have that. Where is it? In your apartment?"

"I—yes." I have no idea. I have no plan.

"We'll just have to get it then. I guess I don't need you anymore."

"Wait—I hid it. You'll never find it. Only my editor knows where it is." I'm talking so I'm still alive. I wanted to stay that way, so I keep talking.

"You'll just have to show us where it is then, won't you?" He stands and moves to the door. He opens it and calls. "Bring the car. We're taking a ride. I'm going to get the girl." Jericho enters the room. Dolby walks up to me. He reaches for the screwdriver. "Oh, and clean up this mess. Bandage him up. I don't want him to bleed all over the car." The Congressman grabs the handle of the screwdriver.

"Don't!" I yell in horror as he yanks the implement out of my leg and chair. I scream. I pass out.

70

I come to in the back of a car. Jericho is behind the wheel, Moe sits in the passenger seat, unmoving. Dolby is next to me. I struggle to focus as the car races through a section of town I don't recognize. I glance over at Dolby. "You're awake. Good. So, do you want to tell me where you hid it?" I struggle to shake my head. It helps clear it. "Well, we'll soon figure out where it is. We're going to pick up a friend of yours. You might enjoy seeing her." Tayla! "I think she might convince you to tell me, hm?"

My blood turns cold. "Don't hurt her."

"You brought this on yourself, you know. If you had listened to me, you wouldn't have to worry about her—and your leg." He pauses to look at my face. "You do seem to run into a lot of bad luck, don't you? What happened to your face?"

"Your thugs beat me up." I manage to spit into his face. The Congressman pulls out a handkerchief and wipes off the spittle.

"You shouldn't have done that." Dolby's face is relaxed, his voice a growl.

"What are you going to do, kill me?" I have no idea what I'm saying. I'm talking to distract myself from the pain.

"That may yet happen. Right now, I'm more concerned about that story."

"I won't tell you where it is." The story didn't exist, but he thought it did. That's was my lifeline until he found out I was lying.

Jericho interrupts. "We have a tail."

Dolby turns and looks out the rear window. "It's just a cab," he says. Cam! My hopes soar.

"Yeah, but he's been following us and he has no fare."

"A friend of yours? Or a cop?" Dolby looks at me.

"I have no idea."

The Congressman addresses Jericho. "Lose him. We don't want any complications." The car speeds up, pushing me into the seat. Dolby looks back. "He's keeping pace. Go faster!"

Jericho glances into the rearview. "Not unless you want to blow out a tire. I'm going as fast as this thing will go."

"Then lose him." Jericho nods and concentrates on his driving. The car takes a turn, throwing Dolby into me. "Watch it!" He pulls a pistol out of an inside pocket. It points at me as if to say, "Don't do anything foolish." I'm too weak from the pain and loss of blood to do anything, much less anything stupid, but for an instant I consider jumping out of the moving car. That may be a last resort. The car swerves again into another turn. The tires screech but hold. This time I'm thrown into Dolby. He pushes me away. The pistol is steady. Jericho passes several cars, weaving between them. Horns blare and tires squeal.

"He's still on us." Jericho is focused on his driving.

"We'll just have to stop him then, won't we? Moe?" Moe glances back at me, then Dolby. He hesitates. "Moe, is there a problem?"

Moe looks at me as if apologizing. He rolls down the passenger side window. He pulls a pistol out of the glove compartment. I take an instant to wonder whether every glove compartment has a gun in it. Shots ring out as Moe fires at the cab. Jericho swerves the car to avoid a truck. "Keep it steady, will you? How do you expect me to aim if you keep throwing me around?" Jericho's response is to throw the car into a right-hand turn into an alley. Moe curses. My mind races to find a way out, but it is blank.

The pain in my leg has subsides to a sharp throbbing. The thick makeshift bandage that is tied around my thigh has begun to soak through. I don't know much about anatomy, but I feel sure the screwdriver cut no major vessels. I shift in my seat, but pain flares up again. I'm not going to do any running for a while. My movement causes Dolby's gun, that had drooped in his hand, back up to me. I freeze. Moe reloads and keeps shooting.

"Got him!" Moe sits back and rolls up the window. "He won't be following us for a while." Dolby, satisfied, nods next to me.

My hopes come crashing down. "You killed him!"

Moe glances at me. "Nah, just blew out a tire." I breathe a sigh of relief.

Jericho slows the car to a reasonable rate. We ride in silence. My brain isn't working. It feels as if it has shut down and gone on vacation. I look out the window and see we have left D.C. Panic rises. "Where are we going?"

The gun still points at my midsection. "Atlantic City."

"Atlantic City? Why?"

Dolby looks over at me. "You won't be telling anyone. The gin and whiskey come in from off the coast there. No laws there. Booze is legal. I have a deal with 'Nucky'. He supplies the booze, I supply pressure in Congress." He waves the gun at me. "Don't worry. You won't be squealing." He pauses, then asks in an off-hand manner, "Where's the story hidden?"

"I'm not telling you." I manage a snarl.

"You're not very smart for a reporter, are you?" I would bristle, but pain and terror keep it at bay. "Why do you think we're going to A.C. instead of your apartment?" I blink but can't come up with a reason. I shrug. "I told you. We're picking up Tayla. You can spare a lot of wear and tear on this car and Tayla if you just cooperate." No wonder I couldn't find her.

"You'll kill us, anyway." I'm certain.

"Perhaps. You're probably right. You may be willing to die, but are you willing to have your girlfriend knocked off?" The Congressman was no better than a hood.

"You should give up. The cops will get you sooner or later."

He laughs. "I'm a Congressman. They can't touch me."

"The Feds can."

"They don't know anything about me. Do they, Jericho?" Dolby glances over at Jericho. "Anyone else following us?"

"No."

"See? I have everything covered. I don't make mistakes. Once I deal with you, I'll be able to get back to business as usual. Make it easy on yourself. Tell me where your story is and I'll make sure you don't suffer." I remain silent and stare at the back of Jericho's neck. The drive is long. At one point Jericho stops the car outside of Philadelphia to refuel, but Dolby's pistol keeps me from breaking free. The Congressman has stopped trying to coerce me. The pain, silence, and loss of blood cause me to nod off several times, only to jerk awake. A wile later, the car drives onto the ferry into New Jersey. This is where Tayla wanted to live. Now, because of me, we were both in mortal danger, and living here seemed like an impossible dream. Now, we would die here–in what looked like the painting she had given me.

My insides complain. "I have to use the bathroom.""Hold it in." Dolby doesn't even look at me, but the gun still points in my direction.

"You don't want me to mess up your car, do you?"

Dolby looks at me, then grimaces. "Pull over." Jericho complies, and the car runs onto the soft sand at the side of the road. "Go with him, Moe. Make sure he doesn't make a break for it." I push the door open.

"Why do I have to go? I don't need to go." Moe looks over the seat at Dolby and me.

"Because I said so. Do what I tell you." The Congressman's voice leaves no room for argument. I shift my legs, and the pain hits me again. I groan. Dolby looks over at me. "Give him a hand. I don't want him messing the car." Moe hops out and moves over to my side. He grabs my elbow and supports me as I stand on my good leg. I clench my teeth as I hop with Moe's help to the side of the road.

"Why are you doing this?" I ask Moe.

"The boss told me to."

"No. I don't mean this. I mean, why are you helping him?"

He shrugs. "He helped me when I was down and out. Jobs are still tough to get. I owe him."

"But he's a thug. He's going to kill me."

"I'm in too deep. I've been with him for years. If I were to cut out he'd kill me too." I finish my business. I consider hopping into the nearby trees, but I wouldn't get far on one leg. "Come on. Time to go." Moe motions me back to the car. He supports me as I head toward my fate. "You're going to let him kill me and Tayla?"

His head snaps toward me. He looks at me for a moment. "Listen! I didn't know he had her. I swear! If I did, I'd–I—I can't do anything." I move to the car and slide into the back seat.

Dolby greets me on our return. "No more interruptions. We should be there in an hour or so. I recommend sitting back and enjoying the scenery. It may be your last chance." He looks out at the pine trees. "It's quite nice here."

71

Jericho pulls the car into the parking lot of a warehouse by the water in Atlantic City, and Dolby signals with his gun for me to get out. I hop my way into the dark interior of the structure. My stomach is in cramps from the stress, and I'm sweating from the pain. Moonlight filters in through dirty windows near the roofline. Moe supports me as we follow Dolby and Jericho. The Congressman flings open a door at the back of the warehouse. Light blinds me for an instant. I gasp as my eyes adjust and I spot Tayla sitting tied on the floor of the cluttered office. She is worn and disheveled. Her eyes grow wide when she sees me, but a gag keeps her from saying anything. Moe, who is still propping me up, flinches.

Dolby pulls the chair out from behind the desk and sits down. He places the pistol in front of him. "Now, isn't this pleasant? We're all here." He turns to Tayla. "I hope my associates have been treating you well?" He looks at her for a moment. "Yes, I see they have." Hate radiates from her eyes. He waves a hand. "Free her mouth. We're all civilized here." Jericho leans down and, with a single motion, pulls the rag that has been acting as a gag from around her mouth. Tayla bursts into a stream of curses and invectives. The Congressman leans back in the chair. It squeaks. "Apparently not all of us are civilized. Gag her, please." Tayla continues her tirade as Jericho replaces the gag. "Much better, don't you think?" He ignores Tayla's muffled expletives. "Your new boyfriend hasn't been very cooperative. Now both of you will suffer. Too bad. You wouldn't be in this situation if you hadn't turned on me." She continues to struggle and curse.

Dolby turns his attention to me. "Now then. Care to enlighten me on where your story is?" I remain silent. "I thought not. That's why we're here after all. I don't like violence but it is sometimes a necessary evil. You do understand, don't you?" He signals to Moe. "Let him go." My mind sees hope, but Moe quickly dashes it when he releases his hold on me. I step on my bad leg. Pain stabs me. I crumple to the ground. I bite back a scream. "Let's try again." The Congressman's tone turns harsh. "Where is it?"

I know the story I hadn't written is the only thing keeping us alive. "I won't tell you." I growl through clenched teeth. Despite being bound, Tayla struggles to her feet and lunges toward Dolby. Jericho pushes her back down by her shoulder. She continues to struggle. He keeps her down. Rage rises in me.

Dolby steeples his fingers on the desk. "You're more determined than I had thought possible. I may have to try harsher methods."

"Let her go!" I scream.

"Or what?"

I have nothing to say. I'm at a loss. I have lost. I'm in no shape to fight or run. I wouldn't since I worry about Tayla.

"This is your last chance. Where is the story?" If I tell him there isn't one, he wouldn't believe me. My only chance is to stall him and hope help comes. It wouldn't. No one knows where we are.

"I'm not telling you."

"You really want to make this difficult, don't you? Jericho, show the young lady the ocean. It's quite romantic this time of night." Jericho pulls Tayla up by her arm. She yelps in pain. I struggle to stand, but my leg gives out again. Tayla kicks and screams through her gag as Jericho drags her to the back door. He pulls it open and pushes her outside.

I break down crying. "Ok. I'll tell you what you want to know. Just don't hurt her."

Dolby nods, then calls after Jericho. The bouncer drags her back into the room. I relax, but I know, at best, I've bought us a brief reprieve. The Congressman gets up from the desk and moves to stand over me. I'm whimpering on the floor, both in pain and in the realization that I've lost. Dolby crosses his arms. "Where is it?"

"I—I have to show you."

"Now don't be stupid. That would mean driving all the way back to D.C. Tell me where it is. I'll call one of my associates and have him check it out. If it's there, I'll spare both of you." I know he's lying. He taps the wound in my leg with his toe. I scream. "Otherwise, you'll suffer and the ocean will have two more burials." My bluff has been called. The only thing I can do is to stall as long as possible.

"It's—it's under the icebox." I'm not sure why I say that, but it seemed like a good place to hide something.

Congressman Dolby nods. "We'll find out soon enough. In the meantime, I want you two to be comfortable. Jericho, tie him up. Make sure they can't get away." I'm quickly trussed and placed next to Tayla. "We'll be back as soon as we can confirm your story. Pray you haven't lied." He motions for his two thugs to follow, then pauses at the door. "Don't go anywhere." Chuckling, Dolby and his two goons leave the room. A short time later, I hear the outer door of the warehouse clang shut.

72

Tayla says something through her gag. I look at her and emotions cascade over me: rage, hate, fear, love, compassion. She repeats what she said. I shake my head, "I can't understand you." She stares at me and says whatever she said louder. It doesn't help. I shake my head again. Exasperated she lies down on the stone floor beside me. I look down at her, not understanding. She moves closer. Her head is beside my hands behind my back. Realization hits. I pull the gag off her mouth.

"Finally!" Tayla struggles then sits up. "It took you long enough." Her eyes probe into my soul.

"I love you too." My response is harsher than it should have been. I relax ."Sorry. I'm in bad shape. But, I do love you."

"What did they do to you? You look like you've gone through Hell." I spend the next couple of minutes recounting the past few days as I struggle to free my hands. "It's my fault you're here. If I hadn't nosed around Dolby and his art show he would have never taken you."

"My poor Randy." She places her head against my arm. "It's not your fault. After he beat me I would have left him anyway. He would have come after me either way. He's insane."

"No. He's sane. He just doesn't care what he does. He's a sadist. Did they hurt you?" Then I remember. "A knife. They found a bloody knife in the apartment. I thought you'd been killed."

Tayla lifts her head and looks at me. Her expression is puzzled. "Knife? Oh! That! I slashed at one of the goons who grabbed me. I didn't do a good job. He's still alive. He's the one who's been watching me."

"Did-did they hurt you?"

She shakes her head. Her dirty mussed hair doesn't flow in waves like I remember but she's still beautiful."No. They just kept me very uncomfortable. I've been tied up and only freed when they feed me and when I need to use the ladies' room."

"How many are there?"

"Just one—the one I slashed. He'll be OK apart from a cut on his arm, darn it." She smiles at me."I missed you. It feels like years since I saw you last."

"I missed you too." I look around. "But we have to get out of here before they get back."

"Why? Won't they let us go when they find the story you wrote? What story were they talking about?"

"There is no story. I made it up. If I hadn't we'd probably be dead."

She gasps. "He wouldn't actually kill us, would he?"

"I wouldn't put it past him. He's capable of anything." I point at my leg.

Tayla glances at my leg and winces. "Does it hurt?"

"Only when I try to use it." I shift my position. My chuckle turns to a groan. Tayla's concern is written on her face. "I'll be OK. I just won't be running out of here any time soon." I clench my teeth and shift again so my back is to Tayla. "Move so we're back to back. Let's see if I can work our hands free." Tayla scuttles around. Our backs touch and a tingle runs through me. My hands feel her hands. I suppress my feelings and pain. I concentrate on the rope that binds Tayla's wrists. The rope around mine chafes and cuts. I find the knot. Long minutes and false attempts later I loosen the knot enough for Tayla to free her hands. She spends more minutes freeing her legs then swings around to face me and soon has my hands are loose. I work on my ankles, but my injured leg makes progress slow.

The sound of the lock on the back door being worked causes us to freeze. Tayla whispers. "It's probably the goon who checks on me." My ankles are still tied. My mind races as I try to form a plan. Tayla gets up and grabs a crowbar from behind the desk. She quickly moves to stand by the side of the door which swings open. A paunchy man stands in the frame. His eyes grow wide in surprise when he sees me. I guess Dolby didn't bother to tell him about me.

"What the?" The man spots my freed hands and moves toward me.

Tayla shuts her eyes and swings. The thug slumps to the stone floor with a grunt. Tayla's eyes open but she stands frozen.

"Tayla are you OK?" I quickly free my ankles. Tayla hasn't moved. I push myself up onto my good foot and hop over to her. "Tayla." Her gaze moves to the sound of my voice. Her stare is blank. "Tayla! It's me! Randy." She blinks and her eyes focus. The crowbar drops to the floor with a loud clang. She breaks down into tears and wraps her arms around me. I fight to stay vertical on my one leg.

"I killed him." She sobs into my shoulder.

I put a hand on her head to comfort her. "No. He'll be fine. He'll just have a nasty headache. You need to work on your swing."

"Are you sure?" She looks up at me. I kiss her.

73

"Well, isn't this cozy?" Dolby's voice causes me to jerk back. "You've been busy while I've been gone, haven't you?" He looks down at the still form of the unfortunate man. "You didn't kill him, did you?" Terrified, Tayla shakes her head. "Too bad. He'll pay for his mistake." I feel sorry for the guy. Moe grabs me by the arm. Jericho moves to grab Tayla but she kicks him in the shin. He pauses half a heartbeat but shrugs it off. She swings her fist at him. In a single motion, he swings her around and wraps his arms around her from the back. She continues trying to kick him.

The Congressman picks up the crowbar. He looks at it. "Is this what you used to take out, poor Pete?" He looks at me.

"I did it." Tayla admits.

"Oh? You're lucky. I don't hit ladies—with crowbars. Get rid of him." Dolby motions to Moe, who winces, then drags the body out of the room. The Congressman replaces the iron rod behind the desk and then sits down. He pulls his pistol out and places it on the desk. My blood runs cold. He must know I lied. "Now then. I've made the call. It will take a while for my employee to check your story. I breathe a sigh of relief. We have a temporary reprieve. "Sit down. I won't tie you again." He points at the pistol. Tayla glances at the gun and stops struggling. My good leg is about to give out so I comply and drop to sit on the ground. Jericho has to push Tayla down before she sits. "Good. Now let's all relax and be friends until I get word about your story." He peers at me.

"I told you where I left it."

"We shall see." He pulls a bottle out of the desk. "Are you thirsty?" I stare back at him. Tayla glares. "No? That leaves more for me." He chuckles. My hands ball into fists by my sides, but I don't do anything else as I steam. He continues, "Your kind thinks it's better than us—that we owe you something. If it weren't for us you'd still be pushing sticks." My blood boils as I glare at the man. He looks over at Tayla. "You really have poor taste in boyfriends. You could have done better... much better." The Congressman shrugs. "It's too late. You're spoiled goods."

Before Jericho can react, Tayla jumps up and lunges at the man behind the desk. His hand moves to the pistol as fast as a snake attack. She freezes in her tracks. "Sit down, please. I wouldn't want to damage you any more than you already have been." I curse him. I curse my leg. Jericho shoves her back down next to me. Moe, who has been standing by the side of the desk, winces. Rage rises in Dolby. "You could have been someone. You could have been a good artist—not great—but good. You blew it. Now, you'll be no one." He stands up. His fists clench. "You betrayed me. You are nothing but trash." His demeanor relaxes. He sits back down. "No matter. I haven't lost anything." He looks over at Moe. "Call D.C. to see if they found anything." Moe nods and leaves the warehouse.

"I really do hate doing this, you know." Dolby sighs. "Being a Congressman is hard enough. You have to make everyone happy. I'm a realist. I know I can't make that happen. So I have to make myself happy. That's really the only thing I can control." He chuckles. He places the pistol back on the desk. He takes another swig from the glass. He turns to me. "Did you vote for me? No? It doesn't matter. It's not like I'll be losing a constituent." He chuckles again. "You'll have to miss the election next month."

"You'll never get away with this." I shift my leg. Rust-brown blood cakes the makeshift bandage. I don't know much about medicine but I know there is a good chance the wound is infected.

Several minutes pass, and Dolby checks his watch. "What is taking so long? Jericho keep an eye on these two. Make sure they don't try to leave without saying goodbye. I'm going to go check on Moe." The Congressman pushes the chair back, grabs his glass, and leaves. Jericho stands, eyeing us. Tayla is fuming but remains silent.

"Why are you doing this?" I ask the bouncer.

"What do you mean?"

"Why are you helping him?"

"He pays good."

I took a stab. "Better than the government?"

His eyebrows shoot up in surprise."I don't know what you're talking about."

"Really? Isn't that a government ring?" I point with a finger at the ring he's wearing on the inside of his hand.

"You're too smart for your own good."

"Does Dolby know?"

"No."

"Are you working undercover?"

"I was. Then the job opened up and I couldn't say no to the pay."

I nod. "So why do you keep the ring then?"

Jericho looks down at his palm. "I like it."

"Why'd you dump me in the river? I didn't have a clue about Dolby then."

My guess is right. Jericho shrugs. "Sorry. I'd rather not say. It's nothing personal on my part. Just money. Everyone has their price."

"No. Not everyone."

"You're trying to buy your life with that story," Jericho responds. I flinch.

"Help us get away."

"Why? So he can put me away instead?" Jericho shakes his head. "No thanks. I like my job and my life."

"Why don't you turn him in then? You must have enough on him to put him away forever." Jericho is about to reply when the Dolby and Moe walk into the office. Dolby's jaw is set. He drops back into the chair. The pistol is in his hand.

"Now then. I have good news and bad news." Dolby doesn't wait for me to ask for one. "The bad news is there was nothing under your icebox. The good news is I won't have to put up with you anymore." He raises the pistol and points it at me. My breathing stops. My brain feels like it's thinking through molasses.

"Wait! My editor probably got it." Dolby hesitates. "I told you he knows where I keep my stories in case I don't check in."

"That would complicate things, wouldn't it?" He waves the gun at me. "I don't believe you. You're lying."

"No. When I don't check in with him every day, he knows something's wrong." I'm making stuff up as fast as I can. "Once the story hits the paper you'll be done. The cops will be all over you."

The Congressman furrows his brows. "They don't know about this place."

"You can't hide forever. The Feds probably know." I glance at Jericho, but I can't read his expression.

Dolby sits down again. "You're desperate." I am. "And you're bluffing." I am. "There is no reason for me to keep you two around any longer. You never had a story. My associate checked your ice box. I also had him tear your place apart." I groan.

I'm clutching at straws that are getting shorter. "The paper should be out in a couple of hours. You'll see. You'll be up a creek without a paddle. It will destroy your bid for reelection."

Dolby's expression drops for a second. I'd scored a hit. "Maybe it's worth waiting until the paper comes out." He spreads his hands in a gesture of magnanimity. "I'm nothing if not a patient man." I breathe a sigh of relief. "Moe, go have Charlie pick up the paper as soon as it comes out. Tell him what we're looking for and have him call us with the scoop, so to speak." Moe disappears from the office. "Now then. Just relax. We'll wait here together, shall we?" He checks his watch. "The evening edition should be out in a couple of hours." The Congressman pours himself another shot. Jericho moves to the only other chair, sits, and leans back on it all the time keeping an eye on us.

I whisper to Tayla. "Are you OK?"

"I'll be better once we get out of here."

I don't want to remind her our chances are slimmer than slim. "So this is Jersey. I liked what I saw when they drove me here. It reminds me of the painting you gave me—it's pretty. I can do without this place though."

She smiles at me. Hope lives again. "I don't like Jersey. There's nothing to do here unless you're in A.C. and the mob runs that."

I'm confused. "Why did you want us to move here, then?"

She tilts her head in Dolby's direction. "To get away from him, of course. I didn't know he had a place here, or I wouldn't have suggested New Jersey." My mind feels like it's full of cotton. "How's your leg?" she asks.

I glance down at it. "I don't know. It's numb. I'm afraid to see what a dirty screwdriver did to it once the bandages come off."

"I'm sorry. I shouldn't have gotten you involved in this mess."

"You didn't do anything. It's my fault for nosing around."

"If I hadn't gotten involved with you, you wouldn't have nosed around."

"I wouldn't trade knowing you for the world. I just wish I could do something to get you out of here." I consider for a moment. "I want you to promise me something."

She looks into my eyes. "What?"

"I want you to promise that if the chance comes up you get out of here and don't wait for me."

Tayla stares at me in horror. "Why would I do that? We'll get out of here together."

"Promise me you'll save yourself if you can." I point at my bum leg. "I can't run with this. Promise."

She shakes her head. "No. I can't leave you behind."

"You have to. It's better you survive than both of us die."

She's horrified. "Don't talk like that. Once the story comes out, he'll have to let us go."

I whisper, "No. I told you. There is no story. It's not coming out. I've run out of ideas. Once he finds out, there will be no reason to keep us around."

"What are you two doing?" Dolby barks at us. "Don't think about trying to escape." I panic that he might have heard me, but realize we'd been whispering and he was just guessing.

"We were just catching up." Tayla's voice is defiant. "We haven't seen each other in days."

"Humph. I wouldn't worry about catching up. You won't be seeing much of each other soon."

"You're vile!" Tayla jumps to her feet.

"Sit down!" Jericho points at the floor to emphasize his point.

Tayla complies, cursing Dolby as she does. He ignores her and takes another sip.

Moe returns. "I told Charlie I'd call him. He said he'd get the rag."

Dolby nods. "Now we wait."

Time grinds to a crawl. We sit. My good leg falls asleep. Dolby drinks.

"When's the next shipment coming in?" The Congressman looks up at the man trying to stay awake in the other chair.

Jericho responds. "Tonight. Whiskey. If the coast is clear. The boat should be in a little past midnight."

"Good. Good." He takes another drink. "I like Atlantic City. They know how to make money. It's an open town, did you know that?" The Congressman's talking more to himself than to us. "No stupid laws about Prohibition. Want a drink? Just have one. Want to buy a drink? Go ahead. No cops or Feds to hassle you." He laughs. "Want to buy a lot of drinks? They'll ship them in for you." The Congressman seems drunk. "That's why I like Atlantic City. It's a fun town. They let business be business. Once I'm reelected, I'll make Prohibition illegal." He laughs again. "I'll make a law that makes booze illegal illegal. Ironic, that's what it is." His glass is empty again. "One day I'll be bigger than Nucky Johnson. He's got this town sewn up." He stares at me. "You. People like you know their place here. It's a good town. It's how it should be." I cringe and seethe but restrain myself. I'm already hanging on by a thread. Tayla just sits and shoots barbs from her eyes, metaphorically . Moe leans against the wall, picking his teeth. He casts an occasional glance at Tayla and me.

Dolby checks his watch. "Moe. The paper should be out. Go call Charlie." The bartender leaves the room. "Now we'll find out if you were bluffing, Mr. Cook." My last name drips disdain.

I glance at Tayla. She's shivering. I whisper. "Are you OK?"

"I'm afraid. I didn't think I would be, but I am."

"Promise me." She looks at me. "Promise me." Her gaze lingers on me, then she nods. I smile. "Good girl. Everything will be fine." She doesn't look convinced. I know I'm not. I gulp. There is no way out once Moe reports the paper hadn't run the story. I mouth. "I love you."

Tayla's smile is weak. "I love you too," she whispers.

Moe comes back into the office. "Boss."

The Congressman looks up from his empty glass. "What's wrong?"

"I called Charlie. There was no answer. I tried twice."

Dolby grunts. "He's probably goofing off again. He's unreliable. I don't know why I pay him. Remind me to have a long talk with him once we get back to D.C." He turns to Tayla and me. "I can't afford to wait any longer."

"You don't want to kill us." I plead.

"Why not?"

"You're a Congressman. You'll be caught." Dolby stares at me, not comprehending. The booze has hit him hard. "Congressmen have to be straight. Once you kill us, you'll be caught and charged with murder." I don't tell him if he doesn't kill us, he'll still be charged with kidnapping. I hope I live that long. He sits. His face contorts as he concentrates. I go for broke. "If you let us go, we'll put in a good word with the Feds." As soon as I utter the words, I know I've made a mistake.

"You won't tell anyone, Blackie." The Congressman's voice drips disdain and hate.

Rage boils in me. I can't hold back. "You goddam—I'm just as good as you! I had to work all my life. My parents were slaves. Your kind took their life away. You used them. They were worth more than your ass. I got my education. I got a job. I worked. I was honest. What did you do? You use people. You hate people who aren't like you. You arrogant bastard." I can't hold back, but I restrain myself and don't vent the way I want to.

Dolby looks at me in surprise. "Who are you to judge? You aren't worth killing. But putting you out of your misery will do me a favor." The gun wavers in his hand. The booze has made him unsteady. A noise grabs his attention. He's not that unsteady. "What's that? Go see." Moe rushes to obey. A few moments later, the door flies open.

"Boss, there are guys outside with guns! Lot of them!"

Dolby stands frozen for a moment, not understanding. "Who are they?" The Congressman snaps out of his confusion.

"Don't know. But I saw at least 5 cars and about 15 guys heading toward the warehouse."

Jericho pulls a pistol out of a holster from under his jacket. "Maybe it's the A.C. mob trying to take over?"

"Maybe." Dolby waves his pistol toward the back door. "We're outgunned, and I can't be caught here. Is the boat outside?"

"No, boss. It's out making making its run, remember?"

The Congressman grunts a yes. "We need a way out."

Before anyone can respond, a voice yells from outside. "We know you're in there, come on out!"

Moe glances around the room like a trapped rat trying to find an escape route. "What are we going to do? There are too many of them."

"We'll have to hold them off until the boat comes in." Dolby glances at his watch. "It's 11. That's an hour."

Jericho shuts the door. "We should hold out here in the office. We can't defend the warehouse. It's too big. The office is close to the dock and we can stick it out here so we can make a run when the boat shows up."

Dolby nods. "Good idea." He looks at his gun. "Save your bullets. We only have what we have."

"Come on out with your hands up or we're coming in!" The voice shouts from outside the warehouse.

"Moe, go out there and take a look." Dolby orders.

"No way, boss. That's suicide."

"Don't argue. Just go out into the warehouse and take a gander at what they're doing. I'm not asking you to go outside." The

Congressman shoves the bartender toward the door. Moe hesitates, pulls it open and disappears from view into the main storage area. I stand, wincing at the pain in my leg. I have to stop Dolby. The gun in his hand swings over to me. "Don't try it." I get back on the floor. Moe returns a minute later. "Well?"

"It's hard to tell. It's dark out. But it looks like they've spread out around the building. We're not going anywhere for a while."

A thundering bang! Another. Then another. "They're breaking into the building," Moe yells.

Jericho checks the load in his gun. "We're going to have to fight our way out."

"We're outnumbered. We wouldn't make it." Moe's voice cracks.

"No matter what happens, get out of here." I whisper at Tayla next to me.

She mouths, "I love you." Her expression is calm, but her eyes tell me she's terrified.

I put an arm around her. "Everything will be OK. Remember your promise." I wish I could believe what I said. The interruption just bought us some time.

I hear footsteps outside the door to the warehouse. Jericho and Moe scurry to shift crates to blockade the door. The voice yells. "We have you trapped. You have no were to go. Drop your weapons and come out and we'll take it easy on you."

"Come on! Out the back! It's our only chance." Jericho runs toward the door.

"But the boat's not back." Dolby's gun points at the barricaded door.

"We can swim down the coast until we're clear of them."

I see Dolby's face grow white. "No. We can't. We can hold them off here."

"Don't be stupid. We're outgunned five to one. The ocean's our only chance." Jericho moves toward the back door. Moe motions at Tayla and me with his gun. "What about these two?"

"Leave them," Jericho instructs. "They'll just slow us down. We won't be able to watch them in the water, anyway." Moe starts toward the door.

"No. I'm not going." The Congressman's terror is palpable. "You're staying here with me." He points the gun at Jericho.

"Why not? Don't be stupid. Swimming is our only chance." Jericho freezes, unsure what to do.

"I—I can't swim."

Jericho considers. "Come on, I'll pull you."

"No. You'll let me drown. I'm not going." The Congressman's voice is firm.

"Suit yourself, but I'll take my chances in the ocean." Jericho turns toward the dock.

"I told you, you're staying with me." Dolby's voice is a low growl. Jericho reaches for the doorknob. A shot rings out and I drop to the ground. The reverberating sound in the small room stuns me. I remain frozen, fearing a second shot. It doesn't come. I peer up from the floor. Tayla is on the ground covering her head. Her face is a picture of terror. I sit up, ready to drop back down if needed. Jericho lays sprawled out on the ground by the door. A pool of blood forms on his back.

"Hold your fire." The voice in the warehouse orders. I realize he's ordering the others with him, not telling Dolby to stop.

The Congressman is frantic. He swivels to point the gun at Moe, who is frozen with his eyes wide. Dolby asks, "You're not leaving me, are you?" Moe shakes his head but says nothing. The Congressman continues, "I don't intend to drown. I'd rather go down fighting than end up at the bottom of the ocean."

"I—I'm not going anywhere." Moe glances at the body. "I'm not big on fish."

Dolby looks over at us on the floor. "Make sure they stay put." His attention focuses back on the door.

"We have you trapped. Come out. We're giving you a minute to come out before we come in."

The voice makes Dolby jump. He yells. "We have hostages. I'll off them if any of you so much as knock on this door." There's no response. "I'm not kidding." He turns and motions for us to get up. Tayla stands. I remain on the floor. "Get up or I shoot her." I glance at Tayla. The look of terror in her eyes makes me ignore my pain. I manage to hop up onto my good leg. I can't feel the other one. Dolby turns his head back to the door and yells. "We're going to walk out of here. No one needs to get hurt. If anyone tries to stop us, I kill both of them." There is still no response. "Moe, clear the door. We're getting out of here." Tayla puts an arm around my waist. I'm grateful for the support. Moe hurries and soon has the door clear of the makeshift barricade. Dolby yells through the closed door. "We're coming out! You don't want to do anything stupid." He turns to us. "That goes for you two as well." He waves his gun at Jericho's body. "Or you'll end up like him."

The voice yells back through the door. "Congressman. Give up. Even if you get past us there's no place to go. No place to hide."

Dolby hesitates. "If you let us walk out of here, I won't shoot them. If you don't, I promise I'll shoot them. Now which do you prefer?" I see the terror in his face fade as he gains the upper hand. I glance at Tayla. I'm supporting her as much as she is me.

There's a minute of silence. "OK. We're backing away from the door. Don't hurt the hostages."

The Congressman waves the gun at us. "You go first. Don't try anything and you'll be fine. Moe, I'll follow you." Moe looks at us. I notice his gaze lingers on Tayla before it moves to Dolby. "What are you waiting for? Get going before they change their mind." Moe motions us to start moving.

I hop leaning on Tayla for support. Progress is slow. I hop into the warehouse. I yell. "Don't shoot! We're coming out!" It takes a few moments for my eyesight to adjust to the dark enclosure. We move toward the front entrance. Moe and Dolby follow close behind, their weapons ready as they shift and glance from side to side.

We walk past crates. I spot a shadow move behind one of them. My nerves are already on edge and now I feel like a jolt of electricity has gone through me. I start. "What's wrong with you?" Moe asks.

"Nothing. Just the pain in my leg," I lie, grateful I'm the only one who saw the figure. My mouth is dry. I gulp and keep moving. I focus on the door. I pray a silent prayer that the two men behind us do nothing to cause a shoot out. We reach the door. I pull it open and hop out into the black night.

74

The cold salt air hits me in the face, the smell of the sea waking me from my stupor. We're outside, but I still don't know what Dolby plans to do or how to escape. A motionless figure stands in the shadow of the building. I feel Tayla shiver under my arm. She is as nervous as I am. I slow down. Dolby pushes Tayla and almost knocks us over. "Keep moving. Get in the car." Moe moves ahead of us to the car that had brought me here and pulls the door open. Tayla eases me in. I move over, and she slips in beside me as Dolby gets into the passenger seat. Moe gets behind the wheel. "Move it," Dolby growls.

The engine roars into life and the car springs forward. Moe glances into the rearview then at the Congressman. "Where to?"

"Anywhere. Just go!"

I glimpse yellow as our car exits the drive that leads up to the warehouse. "You'll never get away with this. They'll catch you," I say as I tap Tayla's arm and point at the car door.

"Shut up. If you open your yap again, I'll dump your body in the Barrens."

Tayla raises her eyebrows and shrugs. She doesn't understand why I pointed at the door. I mouth. "Get ready to jump." Her eyes grow wide in horror. She shakes her head. She mouths back. "No." The car hits the main road at speed, swerving as it does. I fall against Tayla. I whisper. "You promised."

"They're following us." Moe yells as he hits the accelerator.

"Lose them!"

"What do you think I'm doing?" To prove his point, the car hangs a left that slams me into the door. I would have thrown it open and

163

jumped, but I don't want to leave Tayla. The car races down an alley. I glance behind us and see several pairs of headlights. Whoever they are, they are persistent. The car turns onto the main road. The headlights follow. Moe turns. The headlights turn. The game of cat and mouse continues for several miles and the cats don't give up. Dolby checks behind us every few seconds. A few minutes later Moe announces, "They're still behind us, boss, but it doesn't look like they are trying to overtake us. They're just following us." Dolby growls something incoherent in response.

The car turns off the main roads onto the one that leads out of Atlantic City toward Philadelphia. We leave the streets, buildings, and lights of the shore town and drive through the trees of the Pine Barrens. The night is dark, clouds have gathered and obscure the sky. We ride in silence. Dolby continues to check every couple of minutes, which tells me we're still being tailed. Tayla grabs my hand, pressing it. I look over at her. I can only see the barest outline of her features. I give her hand a reassuring squeeze. I had only recently found her, then I lost her. I've just found her again. I would lose her forever if things didn't work out and I couldn't set her free. I have to stop Dolby. I just don't know how.

The trees grow dense the further we drive. We're heading back the way we'd come, but we won't be able to cross back to Philadelphia. The ferry doesn't run this late. I glance at the gauge on the dash and see the dimly lit dial that tells me we will run out of gas before we reach the Delaware. The road, more like a dirt path, this far from Atlantic City begins to wind and curve. Thick trees grow on either side.

"Quick! Pull over and kill the lights." Dolby barks from the front seat, "The trees—get in them. I can't see anyone behind us." Moe swings the wheel and drives the car over the sand that substitutes for soil here. The car slows to a stop amongst some pines. Moe cuts the engine and the lights. I hear Dolby panting as I feel Tayla's warm hand in mine. We sit in the darkness waiting. This is our chance. I have to distract the two in the front seat long enough for Tayla to make a break into the trees. She'd be hard to find in the darkness. I tap her hand. She looks at me in the dark.

Before I can do anything, several cars race by our location. Dolby breaks my concentration and the silence. "We're clear. Head back to the warehouse. They won't think we'd go back there." The engine starts, the lights come on, and the car rolls back onto the firm ground of the road. I see the Congressman check his watch. "The boat should be in by now. We can make a break on it and head down the coast and up the bay to Philly. We can grab another car and get back to D.C. Those goons won't follow us out of Atlantic City." He sits staring at the road ahead. "I thought I had a deal with Nucky. Guess I was wrong. I'll have to figure out another way to get my goods." Any ideas I have of Tayla escaping have gone out the window now that we were moving again. The pressure is off of Dolby. While there was pressure, there had been hope he'd ignore her to save his own skin. Now, I have to figure out something else.

A short time later, we're back on the straight portion of the road. The car is no longer racing and is traveling at a normal pace. Out of the darkness, I hear Tayla whisper. "How's your leg?" Dolby throws a sharp glance at her but says nothing. "I'll live." I whisper then add, "if we get out of this alive."

We continue to drive in silence when Moe warns, "They're back." The car springs forward.

"What?" Dolby swivels to look past me. He curses. "I didn't think they'd catch on that quick."

"Maybe they just gave up and headed back home," I suggest. Dolby glares, but says nothing to me. Instead, he yells at the driver. "Lose them!"

"How? It's not like I can drive through the trees."

"Then go faster!" He continues to stare out the back window. "They're gaining." The pressure is on again as is the Congressman's terror. "Go faster! Go faster! They're still gaining." Moe accelerates the car again. His attention is riveted on the twin beams of light ahead of the car and the trees on either side of the rough road. I glance at the fuel gauge again, hoping we'd run out of gas, but I see we have enough to get us back to the warehouse.

75

"They're gaining! Can't you go faster?" Dolby yells. He is frazzled and focused on the road behind us. The car goes faster. "They—they can't catch me. I'm a Congressman."

I take a deep breath. "Maybe you should let us go. We aren't any use to you know."

Dolby pulls his gun and points it at me. "You. Shut up!"

"At least let Tayla go. You don't need both of us."

"I told you to shut up." The muzzle moves closer.

"Maybe he's right," Moe blurts from the front seat. The gun swings to face Moe.

"Go faster." Dolby looks back past me. "They're still gaining."

"If I go any faster, we'll have a blowout."

"I don't care. Go faster. If we can't go faster, they can't either. I'm willing to take the chance." Moe takes his eyes off the road and looks over at Dolby. "Do it." The gun moves to Moe's temple. He nods and focuses on the road once again. The car lurches forward. Dolby grunts his approval. He glances back. "They're falling behind." He relaxes. The gun drops out of sight as the car races in the darkness, its headlights the only light in front of us. Tayla and I bounce into each other on the back seat whenever the car hits a large bump in the road.

A loud pop startles us. Tayla shrieks. Moe curses. The car swerves to the right. Moe flings the wheel to the left to keep the car straight. The car fights him and wins as it runs off the road onto the sand and slams into a tree. Moe is thrown into the steering wheel. Dolby curses as his shoulder slams into the dashboard. He's lucky. He'd been facing Moe when the car smashed into the tree. Tayla and I are thrown against the seat in front of us, but we are unhurt. The engine dies. Moe lies slumped against the wheel.

I push Tayla against the door. "Run!" I yell. She takes a moment to look at me. That second is enough for Dolby to raise the pistol and point it at her.

"I wouldn't if I were you." He's shaken, but focused.

I groan. She'd lost her chance. The gun shifts its focus to me. "This is your last warning. I swear I'll blow you away the next time." He glances at Moe who hasn't moved. The gun doesn't waver. He turns back to us. "He won't be going anywhere. Now get out and don't try anything." He waves the gun toward the door on my side as he gets out and points the gun at me. I push the door open and slide out onto my good foot. I'm disappointed to see Tayla scooting over to my door and stepping out. I had hoped she'd take the opportunity to run from the other side. I say nothing. "Move," the gun waves toward the trees in the darkness. "They won't be able to track us in the darkness." Tayla wraps an arm around my waist and acts as my support. We move away from the car into the night.

76

"Why didn't you run?" I whisper.

"I couldn't leave you." Tayla whispers back.

"You promised."

"I know. But I couldn't go without you." There's a pause. "Next time. I promise."

We push through the low brush. The sand makes movement slower, but the ground is rain-packed and not the soft loose sand of the beach. "Keep moving. They'll be here any moment. We need to get further from the car." Dolby's voice pushes us to move faster. "Stop!" The sudden order brings me to a sudden halt. "Quiet!" His whisper is a snarl. I strain to hear and make out the sound of footsteps on the sand. Someone is following us. A dark shadow steps out from behind a tree next to the three of us.

"You thought you could leave me." Moe's gun points at the Congressman. There is blood dripping from a gash in his forehead.

Dolby curses, then lowers his own weapon. "You scared the shit out of me. Don't do that again. I could've shot you."

"Why'd you leave me behind?" Moe's gun doesn't waver. "After everything I've done for you."

"Sorry. I—I thought you were dead. You weren't moving."

"I was knocked out. I wasn't dead." I see Moe's gun go back into his jacket. "We should go back to the road."

"Don't be crazy." Dolby relaxes. "They'll be on us any second."

"No. We can't go deeper into the Pine Barrens."

"When I say run, you run." I order Tayla in a whisper. I see an opening as the two argue.

"Why not? We need to lose them. What better way than in trees?"

"We'll get lost. The Devil."

Dolby's voice scoffs. "You're crazy. What are you talking about?"

"The Devil. The Leed's Devil." I can't see Moe's face in the night, but his voice wavers.

"That's just a myth to scare children."

"Run." My whisper to Tayla is emphatic.

"No. I'm afraid." I curse to myself. Another opportunity is lost. I have to figure out how to get both of us free if I'm going to help Tayla.

"It's not a myth. It's real. I had a friend who swears he's seen it," Moe continues.

"Are you a kid? Only kids believe in the Jersey Devil." The Congressman's gun comes up. "No more arguments. We're wasting time. Everyone move. If you want to stay behind, I'll make sure you stay behind permanently." Moe grumbles something I can't make out, but he follows us. He keeps glancing over his shoulder. Dolby snarls, "Keep moving." I feel the muzzle of his gun press against the small of my back. I keep hopping with Tayla, trudging along as she keeps me upright. I try placing weight on my bum leg. There is no sensation and the leg collapses. I stumble, but Tayla keeps me from falling. "Move." Dolby's voice barks behind me. I press on. I break through some more brush and step out on to the road.

Dolby curses. "What the Hell is this?" I spot the crashed car a short distance from where we stand about the same time the Congressman does. There are two other cars next to it and I see a couple of men silhouetted by the headlights. "You've walked us around in circles." The gun comes up to my head.

"I—I didn't know. I couldn't see where I was going." I lie. I had counted my steps, hoping to come out on the road. It had worked.

The Congressman growls, "You've made your last mistake."

A voice calls from the group of cars. "Hey you! Stop!"

Dolby grabs me by the collar and whirls me around fast enough to break Tayla's hold on me. The Congressman throws an arm around my neck. His gun comes up and a shot rings out. He pulls me backwards toward the trees. My heart races. Tayla screams. Moe pulls out his own weapon, but doesn't fire. Shots ring out from the stand of cars. Dolby flinches, then ducks behind me. I fight him, pulling myself toward the cars, but my one good leg isn't strong enough. The bushes scrape against me as I'm forced back. Tayla follows instead of running. Moe is the last to follow. He flinches at the gunshots but doesn't return fire.

Yelling comes from the other side, then the shots cease.

Cursing, Dolby keeps pulling me back further into the trees. A minute later he stops, then shoves me to the ground in front of him. "This is your fault. This is all your God damn fault. We could have gotten away if you hadn't taken us back to the road. You let them catch up." I look up from the sandy soil and see him raise the gun. I say a silent prayer.

"No." Moe's voice barks behind me. "We need him as a shield. We can still use him. If you kill him we're as good as dead."

Dolby pauses to consider. Then the gun waves. "Get up." I comply. I stare down the muzzle. My brain stops working.

"No. Don't be stupid. We need him." Moe's voice breaks through to me. I begin sweating. My heart pounds. My mouth goes dry.

"You're damn lucky, boy." Dolby's voice is quiet and even. "Maybe I won't have to waste a bullet on you. Lord knows you ain't worth shit, much less a bullet." He motions with his head, "Maybe they'll save me the trouble." He chuckles. The area by the road is filled with shouts and orders that grow closer. The gunfire has stopped. "We need another car. We have to get out of here." The Congressman waves the pistol at me. "You. Boy. Go out there and tell them we want one of their cars." Red hate flares in me. My hands clench into fists. "Do it! Or Tayla doesn't see the morning." My focus shifts from the gun to the woman who stands terrified next to me. I force my rage to a manageable level. My body shakes. The gun waves toward the road. "Get going. I'll have my gun on your girlfriend. Tell them. If you do anything else, I'll take her out. I swear." I smile at Tayla. I hope it's reassuring, but she doesn't seem reassured. I begin hopping toward the road. I manage to use my bad leg to keep myself from falling. Dolby's voice calls after me, "She's dead if you don't come back here. Don't waste time either." I don't look back. I have a hard enough time trying to stay upright.

77

I break through the brush and onto the shoulder of the road. A flashlight blinds me. My hands shoot up. My heart screams to get out of my chest. My eyes try to focus through the glare. My mouth is dry, but I yell. "Don't shoot! Don't shoot! Please! Don't shoot!" I'm begging. If I could think straight, I would have fallen to my knees. I don't want to die.

A voice barks beyond the light. "Don't move!" I freeze. Pools of sweat form on my back. Someone, I can't see who, comes up behind me and pats me down.

"I'm not armed." I croak through a dry throat. "I—I'm a hostage."

"He's clean. Keep your hands where we can see them."

"Yes, sir." I was happy to comply. "I'm a hostage."

A familiar voice calls from one of the cars. "He's OK! He's a friend." The flashlight moves off my face but keeps me in the light. A moment later, I hear Cam again. "He's the one I told you about."

The man holding the light speaks. "How d'you get away? How many are there?"

My heart continues to race. "I didn't. He let me go. He wants a car."

Cam asks, "Dolby?"

"Yeah. There are two. Moe and Dolby. He shot Jericho—and Tayla–she's with him."

The man with the light grunts. "We found Jericho in the warehouse." There's a pause. "Come on! We'll have someone look at that leg."

I shake my head. "No. I have to go back. He's got Tayla. He said he'd shoot her if I don't go back. He'll do it too. He's crazy. He wants a car."

"Any idea where he's going?"

"No. Unless it's Philadelphia or D.C. He mentioned those. What's going on? You guys aren't with Nucky, are you?" I look from Cam to the two men and back again. I glance back toward the trees. I don't see Dolby. "I have to go back.

"You can't. If you go back, he'll have more leverage," Cam argues.

My response is immediate. "I have to get Tayla." I hop back toward the trees.

The man who had questioned me says, "Tell him he can have a car. Make sure he takes the one closest to the road." I nod.

"Wait!" Cam calls. I stop. "Want my gun?" He holds up the pistol.

I pause to think. "No thanks. I'd probably shoot my foot off. I'm afraid of guns." I start back to the trees.

One man calls after me. "We'll do our best to get your girl free. Try to delay him as much as possible. If he gets too far from the road or gets in the car, tracking him will be almost impossible." I nod and keep hopping.

78

"Well? Are they going to give us a car?" Dolby's gun points at me. I'm back with Tayla.

"Yes. They said you can have a car."

Dolby sounds jubilant. "I knew they would. They always give in when hostages are involved." He waves the gun at Tayla and me. "You go up ahead. If there's any shooting I want you two to be the ones that buy it." I see him studying me in the darkness. "I don't trust you. You're too clever for your own good. What are they planning?"

My heart skips a beat. "Planning? Nothing."

"You're lying. You were very chatty."

"They—they just wanted to know how many of you there were." I decide lying wouldn't get me anywhere at this point.

"What else?"

"Nothing. I swear. They just said we can have a car—and they'd try to save us."

Dolby stands contemplating. "So it's not Nucky. It's the government. Nucky wouldn't think twice about saving anyone. I wonder who put them on to me." I see the Congressman face me in the night. "You?"

"No—no. I didn't know they were after you."

"No matter. Now that I know who I'm up against, I can use that to my advantage." He signals with his free hand. "Now move. Let's go get that car." Before I can respond, he spins me around and shoves the gun into my back. "Moe, get the girl. Make sure she doesn't try anything." Moe gestures to Tayla to move ahead of him. She complies, but I see she's about to break down in tears. The blood-red sun breaks over the horizon. The scent of the pines is sharper.

79

I've had enough. I let this person ruin my life. He's ruining Tayla's. This has to stop. I take a hop forward, then halt. "Keep moving." Dolby's command is accentuated by another shove in the back.

"No. I'm not helping you."

Dolby shoves me to the ground. A groan escapes my lips. I roll over onto my back. "You'll do as I say."

"Or what? You need me. You so much as said so. You've pushed me around long enough."

"I don't need both of you. She'll help me. You'll help me as well."

"I won't help you." Tayla's voice is almost a whisper.

"You'll both help me." He grabs my arm with one hand and yanks me upright. "You listen up and listen well, boy. You're going to lead us out to that car. If you don't, I'll blow your girlfriend away, right here, right now." Dolby turns to Moe. "Moe, if he doesn't do as I say, shoot her." I can't see Moe's expression in the growing light, but I see his gun droop. Dolby barks, "Now move!" I glance from Moe to Tayla. I'd lost again. I have to find a way to distract them so Tayla can make a break.

I hop out onto the road, with Dolby close behind me. He's shielding his body with mine and even though I can't see them, I hear Moe's and Tayla's footsteps behind us. Dolby's free hand is on my shoulder. He'd be able to sense any movement I make almost as quickly as I would. I glance around and spot several men at the fringes of the trees and around the cars. Cam must be around, but I don't see him. Behind me, Dolby is hyperventilating. He tugs on my shoulder. "Stop." I freeze, but don't know why we've come to a halt. "You!" Dolby calls over my shoulder. "Get away from those cars. We're taking a car. If anyone tries to stop us, they'll be the first to get it." I see the men around the cars hesitate, then move toward the trees. The hand on my shoulder presses me forward. I move forward.

One man yells. "You're not going to get away. Give yourselves up." Several men step forward from the trees. All wield rifles.

"Get back!" Dolby yells. His voice is frantic. The gun waves by my ear. "I'll kill them! I swear!" I cringe. My hands are up. I expect to be shot any moment. I just don't know who is going to do it. "We're taking a car. Move back!" I'm sweating. My heart races. I glance around in terror. There are armed men on all sides. I hear Tayla sobbing behind me. The sound of her crying focuses my mind.

I twist and take a hop forward. Dolby's hand clutches at my shoulder and digs in. I'm ground to a halt before I can recover. The muzzle presses against the side of my head. "Don't even think about it." Dolby's voice is a cold whisper in my ear. He then shouts at the men. "I told you to move back. Now move!" I see the men surrounding us retreat a few steps. Their guns, however, remain poised and aimed at us. We resume moving toward the cars and I continue trying to come up with a plan to free Tayla or delay Dolby long enough for him to be separated from us. I hop as slowly as possible without drawing attention to myself. Dolby continues to hold the muzzle against my head. His breathing is raspy behind me.

A minute later we're next to the cars. The men have watched us but make no move forward. I'm by the car I was told to take.

I take a hop to the car next to it. The gun separates from my head. I grab the handle to open the door. "What do you think you're doing?" I turn to see Dolby's gun pointed at me.

"They—they said we could take this one." I pull the door open.

"I'm sure they did," he snarls at me. "The Feds probably rigged the car somehow. I know how they work." He turns to the car I stepped away from. "We'll take this one." He signals with his gun. "Get in."

"No. I took you to the car like you wanted. I'll do as you say, but you have to let Tayla go."

"I said get in."

"No."

"Moe. If he doesn't get in, shoot her."

I panic, but I stand my ground. "No. I'm not taking a step further until you free Tayla."

Tayla erupts. "No! I'm not leaving you." She rushes to my side and grabs my arm. "Please, I don't want to leave you."

I turn to her. "Don't be stupid. I'm trying to help you."

"He'll kill us whether we help him or not. If I'm going to die, I want to die with you."

"Isn't this just wonderful?" Dolby snaps. "Two lovebirds willing to die for one another." His gun comes up. He grabs Tayla and yanks her away from me and shoves her toward the car. "Get in."

Tayla spins her back to the car. "No. I'm not going anywhere with you. You're scum—and a coward." Dolby slaps her with his free hand. I see Moe flinch. The bartender's hand clenches his gun.

Dolby takes a step forward. A shot rings out. I hear it whiz by between the Congressman and me. The four of us drop to the ground. I see the men around us move closer. They have used the argument to adjust their positions.

Dolby fires a shot over the car. One of the men drops to the ground. Shots ring out all around us. Dolby and Moe fire off a couple of shots each. Then Dolby yells. "Moe, stop shooting. Save your ammo. They're trying to get us to waste it." He peers over the hood of the car. I glance at his face. He's sweating and his face is red. His gun moves from target to target. His eyes glance around. He looks like a trapped animal searching for a way out.

80

Dolby ducks back behind the car and pulls the door open. The gun motions us to get in. "Get in, boy. I'm going to shoot her if you don't." I've had enough. My blood boils. My hands ball into fists and I lunge at the Congressman. Caught off guard, he is thrown back and smashes into the fender of the car with an "oof". The gun drops from his hand onto the sandy soil. I smash a fist into the side of his face. Stunned, he tries to focus. I follow up on my advantage by swinging again. This time he ducks, and I hit air. He grabs for the pistol but I slam my shoulder into him. Cursing, he swings and knocks the wind out of me. I suck in air and grab his neck. I squeeze. I'm not thinking. I'm trying to survive. His face turns red. His fingers claw at my hands as he struggles to breathe. I press harder. His knee comes up. It connects, and I collapse onto my side in pain.

I see Dolby slide down the side of the car onto the ground as he fights to breathe. Moe and Tayla crouch near us, away from any potential gunfire. Dolby recovers faster than I do. He reaches over and retrieves the gun. He pants as he rubs the growing bruise on his face. The gun points at me. "You'll pay for that. You should've learned your place." I manage to curse and spit at him. I'm too far to hit him.

A voice yells from behind the cars, pulling his attention away from me. "Give up! You have no place to run. We have the road blocked off. Throw out your guns and come out with your hands up." Dolby curses and blindly fires a shot over the hood of the car. Shots fly above us. One shatters the windows, throwing a cascade of shards onto us. Dolby curses again.

I pant, "You've lost." My pain has subsided and I sit up. "You can't get away." I look over at Tayla. Her eyes are wide as she crouches between Dolby and Moe. She's terrified. I'm just as terrified.

Dolby puffs air. His face is bruised and scratched and his glance is furtive. It fastens on me. "You! This is all your fault. If you hadn't meddled in my affairs, I wouldn't be in this mess." He sucks in more air. "I had it made. Everything was working fine. You! You did this." His voice is frantic as his desperation and frustration grow.

"This is your last chance. Throw out your guns and come out with your hands up. This is your last warning."

"If I have to lose it all, you'll lose too."

Everything moves in slow motion. His gun comes and I see his finger compress the trigger. I scream. "Tayla!" She lunges toward me.

Moe yells, "No!" The bartender's gun comes up, and he fires. There are two thunderclaps as the shots ring out. Tayla is spun around by the impact of both bullets and drops to the ground in front of me. I howl and lunge at Dolby. His face is a mask of glee. My bad leg collapses under me as he fires another round. It screams above me. Moe fires again. The Congressman's eyes grow wide in surprise. He stares at the hole in his chest then crumples.

Men, with guns drawn, swarm around us. Cam runs up behind them but freezes when he sees the scene. The gun drops to the dirt from Moe's limp hand. He stands stunned staring at Tayla. I pull myself to Tayla, who lies on her back. The sand turns red as it absorbs her blood. I lift her head and place it on my lap. Her eyes flutter open. Her breath is shallow and rasping. I'm sobbing like a little kid. "Why didn't you run? Why did you do that?" Tayla's eyes focus on me. She smiles, then with a deep breath, closes her eyes. I cradle her head and wail.

81

I feel a hand on my shoulder. I look up through a haze of tears and see Moe crouching next to me. "I'm sorry, boss. I know she was special to you." I nod and the weight of the pain in my heart threatens to crush my chest. "We should go. Let the Feds do their job."

"Give me a few moments. I need to be with her." I look down at Tayla in my arms.

"It's time. You've been sitting here crying for the past half hour." I'm stunned. I glance around and spot Moe, who is handcuffed and sullen next to someone, asking him questions and taking notes. Dolby is slumped against the car where he had been shot. A large red splotch stains the front of his suit. Someone is walking around taking photographs. Several men stand around the cars. They don't look relaxed. Others are going through the car against the tree.

"Thirty minutes?" Not quite comprehending, I look at Cam.

"Yeah, boss. We need to go. The coroner needs to take photos and do his job."

"No!" I scream. "I'm not leaving her."

"She's gone, boss. You can't help her now." Moe's comment stabs at me. I wipe the tears from my eyes. Moe's presence is reassuring. He continues, "Come on. It's time. Let them do their job. You're going to hurt, but you have to let her go." In the back of my shredded mind, I notice the toothpick is missing.

My voice is a whisper. "I don't want to. I just found her. I tried to save her but she wouldn't let me." I break down into tears.

Cam stands. "She loved you." He considers for a moment. "Maybe some people don't want to be saved." He glances at the Congressman.

"Some people aren't worth saving. Let's go."

I look down at Tayla and gently place her head on the ground. The sand around her body is almost black from the blood it has absorbed. "I love you. I always will." She still has a faint smile on her face.

—

I spend an hour sitting on the sand recounting what I could remember over the past weeks, starting with my meeting Tayla. That was the first, this was the last. I'm exhausted. I hurt. My soul hurts. I tell the agent everything I know about the bootlegging and the Klan robes and where to find them. I also tell them where to find the list of names of fellow Klansmen I found under the blotter. The man nods and says he has no more questions. I note the ring he wears on the inside. My mind doesn't make a connection.

I look at where Tayla lays covered with a sheet. Several ambulances and police cars have arrived and medics are standing around or talking to the Feds. Dolby's body is likewise covered—he doesn't deserve even that.

Cam interrupts my thoughts. "You're still alive. That's something to be thankful for." I don't respond. I don't feel thankful. I feel numb. "They say you can go if you want."

I glance at the white-wrapped body on the sand. "I don't want to." I feel empty. The emptiness will never be filled.

"I'm in no rush. But I'm here if you need a cab." I acknowledge Cam with a nod. I'm thankful for his support.

I spot Moe being led to one of the cars. His head is down, his expression morose. I had to know.

"Wait up!" I called to the agent who was helping Moe into the backseat of a car. I hop over.

"Why? Why did you shoot Tayla? What did she ever do to you?"

Moe flinches, then looks at me in pain. "I—I didn't mean to. I—I shot at Dolby. She got in the way." There's a pause. "I—I loved her even though she wouldn't give me the time of day. I thought Dolby was aiming at her when I shot." I didn't know. The Fed opens the door. Moe slides in. "I'm sorry."

I'm confused. My mind is slow. "About what?"

"I paid Jericho to warn you off of Tayla. You two looked too cozy that first night. I–I wanted her. I had no idea he'd go that far." I blink, uncertain what to say. "He was supposed to scare you, not dump you

180

in the river. I just wanted a clear field. I'm sorry." The car window rolls up, and the car roars off the sand, onto the road, and out of sight.

I lean against a car. I'm exhausted. Cam sits on the hood next to me. "Cam, how d'you end up here? I don't get it?"

"After I had my tire blown out chasing you, I went to the police—there was a sergeant there that seemed skeptical at first. I convinced him you weren't making stuff up. They set up a stakeout at your place and got someone who was going through your stuff. They tailed him to his place and when he got caught, he spilled everything he knew. He said he was looking for a news story you'd written. The cops called in the Feds once he told them you were in A.C."

I nod. "I didn't have a story then. I have one now."

Moe looks over at me. "We all done here? Need a ride to the hospital? It looks like the ambulances have left." I glance and see Dolby and Tayla are gone. She would never be gone from me.

I look down at my leg. I nod. "Sure. Let's go." I stand and try my leg. It still can't hold my weight.

"I guess everything is settled." Moe hops off the hood. "What next?"

I waver, balancing. I look at the rising sun amongst the thick trees. "I still don't understand why I got clobbered—by the two Feds."

Moe gives me his elbow for support. "I asked about that. It turns out they had a man on the inside investigating the Congressman. He went rogue."

I nod, "Jericho."

"They wanted to nail both him and Dolby. They thought you were a new member of Dolby's group, so when they had the chance they grabbed you. They believed being new you'd be easy to break and scare off before you did something you might regret. They wanted you to spill the beans on Dolby, or at least get out of their way." I grunt acknowledgment. "Anyway, they've been investigating the club and the bootlegging for a while. They heard rumors Dolby was involved but they had no proof—until you gave it to them just now."

"Little good it will do them now. He's dead, and good riddance." I want to spit, but my mouth is dry. "Let's get to the hospital. I can use a rest." I look around. "Where's the yellow?"

Cam points up the road. "That ways a bit. They didn't want me getting in the way. Wait here. I'll get it." Cam jogs up the road and around a curve.

82

Several days later I'm back home in D.C. The apartment is as I left it. My leg is sutured and I'm infection free. My bad luck. I hobble around on a crutch until the muscle and wound heals. I'm glad to be home. I look around the place. I've hung up and put away most of Tayla's belongings. My heart breaks again and I feel empty. I pick up her robe from the top of the bureau where I'd left it. I bring it up to my face and inhale. What few memories we had together rush back. The tears return as well. I walk past her painting that now so much looked like the Pine Barrens. I reach to rip it off the wall, then stop myself. I drop onto a kitchen chair and sob.

The coroner had finished his job, and they would hold the service this weekend. I'm not sure if I'd survive it. The robe absorbs my tears like her blood on the sand. I sit for a long time, I'm not sure how long. I get up and move to the kitchen table. I have an actual story to write.